THE
SHARP
EMPIRE II

THE SERPENT STRIKES BACK

TYLER JOHNS

Order this book online at www.trafford.com
or email orders@trafford.com

Most Trafford titles are also available at major online book retailers.

Printed in the United States of America.

ISBN: 978-1-4669-8807-1 (sc)
ISBN: 978-1-4669-8806-4 (e)

Trafford rev. 04/02/2013

 www.trafford.com

North America & international
toll-free: 1 888 232 4444 (USA & Canada)
phone: 250 383 6864 ♦ fax: 812 355 4082

CONTENTS

THE TRUTH OF THE FOES

This all began with the earthly animals that were once humans' pets or wild/endangered species, in which mainly mammals were humanized by Celestial glory, causing them to walk on their hind limbs. They created the Heaven Federation. Their enemies were monstrous, dinosaur-like reptiles, birds of prey, and even therapsids that were originally extinct but brought to the present. These beasts were part of the Sharp Empire run by the evil emperor, Hieronymus Sharp, who was once a cobra but grew limbs for walking, standing, and grasping. His knowledge was great and powerful to the ultimate.

The animals of the Heaven Federation acted just like human astronauts. The first heroine was a lioness named, Nala Boomer, but she was executed as she was accused having not enough courage to fight the Serpentials. Her partners Skinamarinky-Dinky-Dink Skinamrinky-Doo, an orangutan with the reincarnation of a popular children's song, and Zinger Warsp, an oversized wasp, still lived. They hired new heroes, including: Captain Tiblo Tigro, a tiger nearly hunted but survived; Shana Cargon, an inventive kangaroo banished from her herd; Manda Monka, a wolf from another planet whose world was threatened with her family murdered; Martino Izodorro, the Irish human farm boy brought to space by Skinamar and Zinger after Martino lived with his aunt and uncle on their farm; and finally, Regulto Beauxon, a medical scientist from a British father and French mother, who invented a potion that would conquer his fears, but it turned him into a beast named Rufus.

The Serpentials once kidnapped Martino's younger sister, Princess Mariana Izodorro. But she was rescued by the Heavenly Federal forces that made her *their* princess. She and some spies were sent to steal the plans for the Sharp Empire's biosphere and ultimate weapon, the Death Scale, but the emperor's most trusted advisor, Darth Waternoose, was sent to get the plans back. The Serpentials decided to execute the princess by drowning her in the Death Scale's hollow lake called, Lake Prisoner. So they did that before the freedom fighters could rescue her.

The freedom fighters were confronted by the celestial white condor, Artidector. He said that he and his children would revive the princess while she is frozen in a prism of ice frozen from Lake Prisoner, hovering like a satellite.

The freedom fighters were built one-piloted ships by Artidector who also gave powers to them. The freedom fighters gained strength and courage to fight the Serpential forces and the emperor's henchmonsters. As they escaped the Death Scale, they went to their home base in the horse head of the Orion Nebula. As the Heavenly Federal pilots got ready, the Death Scale moved close to the horse head. The Heavenly Federal pilots had to fight to destroy the Death Scale before it could destroy their home base. The freedom fighters in their new ships had to help fight until Martino shot the torpedoes into the Death Scale's north pole, which blew the Death Scale up into four major pieces including tiny asteroid particles within.

But the entire war was not over. It was just the beginning.

CHAPTER 1

FICTION FINDERS

It is a dark time for the Heaven Federation, although the Death Scale had been destroyed. The Sharp Empire plans to eliminate all dream worlds and a group of freedom fighters headed by Captain Tiblo Tigro must stop another battle from happening. They hide in a hidden base on a newborn planet of ice. The evil lord, Darth Waternoose, has sought the time of all things that were never meant to happen. And so the war continues . . .

Our story continues with the Serpential forces finding things that would not exist in the real world. On the northwestern quarter of the Death Scale and in the city of Serpentopolis, in the Palace of Sharp, the emperor sought some constellations with stories told from children's television on Earth.

"The sun sets in the sky," he said. "Teletubbies say goodbye." He pressed a button on the arm of his throne. He spoke through a tiny microphone and said, "Fire at will!"

Officers obediently activated the Death Scale's firing system in the palace's basement. Then the four spires, one at the far end of each building, shot the lasers at the mechanical eye at the top of the palace. The eye shot a larger laser beam, as it absorbed the smaller beams, at where the hidden realm mentioned the television series of "Teletubbies".

A moment later, a message started to beep on the throne's arm. The emperor pressed a button that turned on the communication system with holograms. The hologram appeared as an old cassowary, the Serpential marshal, Martopher MacFnurd.

"I have located the Heaven Federation's new base," said the marshal.

"Excellent," said the emperor.

"And we have eliminated six series from children's television," said the marshal.

"Very good," said the emperor. "Emperor Sharp out." He turned off the communication system, and the marshal's hologram vanished.

Meanwhile, the Serpential forces followed the direction to the new Heavenly Federal base, riding in scale cruisers large and grayish green. Scale destroyers were large, long, thin, arrowhead-shaped ships with large super-charged laser cannons on the sides, able to destroy anything in their path. The largest ships were scale carriers: massive dark blue ships, shaped like a pizza slice and twice the size of the blue whale.

Three cruisers, two destroyers, and one carrier were shooting floating asteroids in their path with their laser cannons. New star elements appeared on these rocks in creation of a new star system.

"We'll find those enemies of ours soon," said the Serpential general, Karchong Fang, a large four-armed monáchi (a therapsid type of beast with the traits of a strong gorilla and a tyrannosaur).

"I, as a specialist," said the Serpential admiral, Marwick MacFnurd, who is another cassowary and the marshal's brother, "will seek their purpose and plan a capture." He had a right bionic eye that was a shining red horizontal slit with a white frame over the connection to the socket. He decided to show himself clever to his work.

A moment later, pirate knights brought a glass jar with an alien type of pixie. They also carried crates with the emperor's new monstrous creations. They showed them to the head force officers.

"We have new plans from the emperor," said Major Gliff, a blue-green bipedal lizard pirate knight.

"Keep those closed," said General Fang, "or else they go wild."

"Those are now useful to destruct our enemies," said Admiral MacFnurd.

"It's our chance," said Major Gliff.

"I've got our schedule," said Private Frash, a short, hooked beaked hawlkon pirate knight (a bird of prey part hawk and part falcon).

"We should approach after a while as we find those H.F. creatures," said Sergeant Hawkeye, a long beaked bird of prey with a left global bionic eye.

Suddenly, a security camera lit a laser beam at the glass jar with the alien pixie. Major Gliff got distracted. He snarled and shrieked by his throat as he dropped the jar which hovered toward the ceiling and then fell to the floor and broke. The pixie escaped. The alarm beeped aloud among the halls of the carrier.

"Emergency maneuvers!" shouted the general.

Marshal Martopher MacFnurd called the scale troopers through a speaker on a nearby dashboard, "Troops! We have fugitive specimen raging about!"

A group of scale troopers detected the halls. Then one of them found a flying insect-like creature, which was the pixie. It flew up to a nearby vent, breaking it open with its flaming power. The scale troopers followed it there.

"Security risk! Coming to bridge!" said one of the troopers through his wrist speaker.

"It's coming this way!" said the admiral, looking at the locating computer.

"It's heading for the power generator!!" the general shouted. He grabbed one of his blasters and shot at nearby pipes repeatedly, looking for the pixie. As the pixie reached the generator a glitch occurred throughout the carrier's power system, playing a song that went:

"If we listen to each other's heart
We'll find we're never too far apart."

"Somebody, turn that off!" shouted the general as the song continued:

"And maybe love is the reason why, for the first time ever we're seeing it eye to eye."

A pirate knight turned it off by a power switch. The locating computer showed the pixie lying dead by the power generator. After a moment of accuracy, the Heavenly Federal base had finally been located on the computer.

"A-ha," said the admiral as he found the base's location on the computer nearby. "Deploy the hidden monsters in satellites!" He commanded the scale troopers. So they carried crates with the emperor's hidden creations in satellites being deployed, dropping the crates inside them through suction tunnels. The satellites were launched to the new cold planet far ahead of the scale ships.

After many miles traveled to that planet, the satellites entered the atmosphere using saw wheels to cut open the crates and lifting a floorboard by a crank to dump them. Inside the crates were elliptical webs with red balls in the middle. They fell to the snowy ground. They were pods of monsters burrowing into the ground called thumblers, slim, lizard-like, red monsters with heat vision and slim arms with sticky hands with lots of fingers that come out of the ground seeking their prey by catching it and spewing lava out of their mouths. As they rose out of the ground, their hot bodies melted some of the snow away to form their burrowing circles. The Serpentials had decided to set a trap for their enemies.

CHAPTER 2

MARTINO IS MISSING

As the thumblers used their powerful hearing senses to hear a distant enemy from far away, they burrowed into their holes. From that distance came a person in a heavy Eskimo-like coat, riding on a robotic camel in a blizzard that just ended. It was Martino Izodorro. Under the coat's hood his face was covered in a blue, ninja-like mask with large goggles protecting his eyes. He stopped for a moment when a message beeped on his wrist communicator. He pulled away the arm of his coat, wearing thick brown gloves, and pressed the button to answer the message.

"Mr. Izodorro," said the hologram that appeared after the button was pressed. It was General Gando Grizzle of the Heaven Federation, a big grizzly bear. "There won't be any shelter for you out there as you return to our base."

"I'm alright," said Martino. "Something's fishy out here. Martino out." He turned off the communicator. The robotic camel beeped and howled.

"Whoa! Hey!" Martino shouted. "Steady there, boy. Hey what's the matter, you smell something?"

Suddenly, a white crocodile came from a nearby frozen pond and roared in anger. Martino quickly jumped off the camel and took out one of his father's digital disk launchers that Zinger gave to him back on his home planet. He shot at the ice crocodile that approached the robotic camel. The crocodile bit at the camel's leg and pulled it off. Martino ran off as the camel fell to the ground it slowly exploded. Martino headed for the area with bare circles within the snow. He tried to approach one of the circles but the circles had the thumblers in them. As Martino tried to think of a fire to build, a thumbler came out of the nearest circle. It grap-pled onto Martino's leg with its sticky hands and splattered tiny drops of lava from its mouth. Martino screamed. The lava burned part of his thick fur trousers. He wiggled himself free and the thumbler released him. Martino figured that the barren circles had those creatures in them. So he found a snow cave many yards away. So he ran to it in thick snow. Thumblers shot balls of hot lava and Martino dodged them, heading for shelter.

Meanwhile in the hidden Heavenly Federal base under the cold sea a few miles away, the Heavenly Federal forces lost contact with Martino. Captain Tiblo Tigro of the Heaven Federation stood by his sturdy ship, the Great Red Shark, testing communication with Martino, but the system failed. So he made contact with General Gando Grizzle.

"General," Tiblo said as he got himself and the general to face each other's holograms with his communicator. "My human partner is out of contact. I think his communicator malfunctioned."

"I made contact with him a while ago," said General Grizzle, "he said he was all right."

"I should find him out there," said Tiblo.

"Peace will be with you," said the general. "That's the blessing."

"Actually, if you want to make peace, you got to give it all you've got."

"Yes indeed." The general laughed.

"Captain Tigro out." Tiblo turned off his communicator. "How's it coming up there?!" He called up to the orangutan, Skinamarinky-Dinky-Dink Skinamarinky-Doo, who was drilling screws into new parts of metal on the back of the Great Red Shark.

"It's nearly done," Skinamar said.

Tiblo got another message beeping on his communicator. He pressed the button to answer it. It was Shana Cargon, the kangaroo mechanic of the freedom fighter crew.

"Tiblo," she said after her hologram appeared. "How should I stand using a bathroom in a diaper?"

"That's how it's supposed to be," said Tiblo. "Keep the gear on. We're on another planet, so get used to the idea."

"Any diaper with excrements bothers me often," said Shana.

"If it's bothering you," said Tiblo, "change it!" He quickly turned off his communicator before Shana could say another word. "God I hate the way she behaves," he said.

"Probably shouldn't have kept her," said Skinamar, "especially after training her." He kept working on the ship.

"I'll go check on the others," said Tiblo. He exited the hangar and headed through a white hallway and entered a room where some militias were working.

"Ah, Captain Tigro," said the Heavenly Federal Colonel Starp, a bluish gray maned wolf.

"I'm here for my scouts," said Tiblo.

"Sure, go ahead," said the colonel spreading his paws away from his sides. Tiblo went to Regulto Beauxon by the other side of the wall. Regulto wore a white overcoat for the cold outside. He worked on a computer for research.

"How's it coming, Reg?" asked Tiblo.

"Well, by nothing really," said Regulto. "We can have an enemy by tomorrow." He found the research of the Sharp Empire's schemes as approaching the base.

"Something's wrong with these computers," said Tiblo. He went to Manda Monka, now dressed in a dark blue tunic and violet trousers.

"How about you, Manda?" Tiblo asked her.

"There seems to be a prophecy about us under attack," said Manda as she did the same computer research. "That's what these computers are telling us."

"I just wanted to make sure it's not mushy nonsense by feminism," said Tiblo. He left the research room out the door.

Manda suddenly had a thought. She made a suspicious facial expression. Her ears on tip twisted a bit. She stared at the doorway. She went out of the room and went to Tiblo.

"Tiblo!" she called.

"Now what do you want?" Tiblo asked as Manda confronted him.

"Tiblo we need you," said Manda.

"What for? I got to find Marty out there."

"This prophecy is real. Our enemy *is* coming for us."

"When they approach our base, we'll be ready for them." Tiblo left through the hallway back to the hangar bay. As he got there he decided to rent a submarine. He went to the pressure-affected pool nearby the side. A security camera focused on Tiblo. It said, "Your identification?"

"Captain Tiblo Tigro," Tiblo said to security.

"Permission granted," said the camera as it turned off.

Tiblo jumped in a gray miniature submarine. He jumped into the cockpit and started the engine.

"Here I come, Marty," he said.

The doors opened for the sub. Tiblo steered it out through to the open water.

CHAPTER 3

TIBLO SAVES MARTINO

Meanwhile, Martino slept in the cave he went in for shelter until suddenly, he awoke. He was barely able to get up on both feet. He still felt tired. He grabbed his disk launchers out of his backpack pointing them at the ceiling if any thumblers intrude from above. Suddenly, a thumbler slid down through the ceiling and Martino shot it as the thumbler spewed lava like a waterfall. It created a hot pool of lava settling within the floor. Martino escaped around it and ran to the other open end of the cave. As he exited, he felt his legs allowing him to kneel to the snowy ground, and then he suddenly reclined to it, lying face down. Suddenly, a white figure of light appeared. It was Artidector. He spread his giant white wings and stared down at Martino, lying asleep.

"Martino!" Artidector called to him.

Martino lifted his face slowly up to Artidector.

"Arti-dec-tor?" he said in a mumbling tone of voice.

"You will seek the mystical gem scales," said Artidector, "the artifacts used to hold the Death Scale together." He disappeared and the light around him vanished.

Suddenly, Tiblo appeared riding on a robotic rhinoceros that he found in the sub he rented. He rode the rhinoceros to where Martino lay. Tiblo had worn a heavy Eskimo-like coat with a warm blue mask that covered his face and his muzzle going through a large hole in the middle. He jumped off the rhinoceros and walked to Martino. He dragged him over by the rhinoceros. Then he looked at him by turning him over.

"Artidector . . ." Martino said still resting in the cold. "Gem . . . Scales . . ."

Tiblo placed his paws on the sides of Martino's face.

"It's gonna be all right, Marty," he said. "Just relax."

Suddenly, the rhinoceros malfunctioned with a moaning yawn. It fell to the snowy ground. Tiblo shot it with one of its blasters that he got out of his backpack. The rhinoceros caught fire from the explosion in its circuits. Then Tiblo dragged Martino to the fiery wreckage to stay warm by that fire. He decided to use it for a campfire. He and Martino warmed up. Martino slept.

As Tiblo kept the fire going, a swarm of flying electrical objects with axe-like jaws with zigzag tops and bottoms of headed monsters floating in the air called thunderheads; these bodiless head creatures could zap lightning from their mouths. As they reached to the surface from the atmosphere, shooting their lightning, Tiblo used his blasters to shoot each one at a time. The thunderheads sparked with lightning surrounding their heads. They shook and vanished. Tiblo kept his eyes on Martino by the wreckage fire.

CHAPTER 4

WATERNOOSE'S UPGRADE

Meanwhile, back in space on the scale carrier, the evil crab-like, robotic lord, Darth Waternoose stared at the stars out the window. Suddenly, a message beeped on his wrist communicator. He answered it.

"Lord Waternoose," a hologram appeared and said. It was Admiral Marwick MacFnurd. "Your upgrade is ready to install." The hologram vanished.

Darth Waternoose walked his six crab-like legs down the walk between aisles of laser cannons. As he did, he entered a room with an operational table. Waternoose lay on his back on it. Admiral MacFnurd grabbed an upgrade of six robotic tentacles forming a ribcage from a robot. Darth Waternoose opened his front belly cabinet. The surgeon droids—floating robots with probe-like tools to operate any patient specimen available on the table—

started to cut open Waternoose's sides and lift up all the cabinet shelves. They placed the robotic tentacles on a bar within the space where the human body's belly showed.

Soon the upgrade was nearly installed. The surgeon droids screwed the bar with tentacles inside the open space with drills. They placed the shelves carefully back in place, drilling them back in the cabinet. Waternoose lifted himself off the table, standing back on his six jointed legs. He decided to test his upgrade, opening his belly cabinet and allowing a tentacle with a three-pronged grasping end to slither out.

"Excellent work," said Waternoose to the surgeon droids. Waternoose exited the room and walked back toward the window he was standing by in the first place. A moment later, a message beeped on his wrist communicator. He answered it. A quadrilateral of different holograms appeared. There was General Fang and Marshal Martopher MacFnurd.

"What is it, General?" asked Waternoose.

"Lord Waternoose," said General Fang, "our monster traps have worked and we almost caught one of our enemies."

"We're getting as close to our planned strategy as possible," said the marshal.

"We'll yet be ready for them," said Darth Waternoose. He turned off his wrist communicator, thinking about the next battle plan, seeking the future with his top left eye.

CHAPTER 5

CARPOON

Suddenly, some of the militias witnessed an unknown ship on the monitor screen. It was shaped like a parrot-beaked dinosaur's head. It was just ¼ of a mile from the scale carrier. Admiral MacFnurd grabbed a speaker system and activated it, saying, "Your flight is restricted for only if you are anything we know of or perhaps you should or may join our forces."

The pilot in the ship was dressed in a pirate knight's suit of armor. He was a shell-less turtle.

"I am a new Serpential," he said. "The emperor has chosen me. I am a bounty hunter."

"We must see your ship aboard," said the admiral.

"As you wish," said the bounty hunter. He flew his ship to the underside of the carrier where a hatch opened to the docking bay. The Serpential officers and scale troopers went down to the bay to confront the ship.

"Step off of your ship by post-haste!" the admiral commanded. The pilot stepped off to show himself.

"I'm Carpoon," he said, "shell-lacking turtle bounty hunter. I've been authorized to help you catch those freedom fighters."

"Did the emperor really accept you?" asked General Fang.

"Yes indeed," said Carpoon.

"You are welcome to help catch our enemies red-handed," said the admiral.

"The emperor wishes you to seek their purpose," said the marshal.

A message beeped on Carpoon's wrist communicator. He answered it.

"How's my specialist?" asked the hologram that appeared. It was the emperor.

"I'm already aboard," said Carpoon.

"Do you have all of your supplies?" asked the emperor.

"Yes I have everything."

"Excellent."

"Carpoon out." He turned off his communicator.

"Our empire is as strong as ever," said Major Gliff, smiling.

And so, as Carpoon was hired, he was demanded to use his bounty detector for the freedom fighters of the Heaven Federation, and the new plan was coming true.

CHAPTER 6

FREEDOM FIGHTER
REUNION

Back on the cold planet as Tiblo and Martino remained
stranded in the snow, Heavenly Federal ships flew from the
hidden base underwater and flew up to the sky. They all
headed for the snowy landscape to find the missing heroes.
Each ship contained two pilots sitting next to each other.
The ships were known as the Rough Squadron. A male
canine pilot in Rough 4 made contact with the base as he
searched for Tiblo and Martino.

"Come in, Water Base," he said. "This is Rough 4.
This is Rough . . .4." He decided to make contact with the
missing heroes.

"Mr. Izodorro," he said," do you copy? This is Rough 4."
He tried another thing.

"Captain Tigro," he said, "do you copy? Do you co-
freaking-py?!"

"We're over here!" Tiblo called the pilot back. The pilot smiled.

"Water Base," he said. "This is Rough 4. I found them. Repeat? I found them." He flew around where he found Tiblo and Martino in front of the wreckage of the broken robotic rhinoceros. He dropped a ladder from a hatch on the underside of his ship. Tiblo and Martino grabbed onto it facing each other from each opposite side of the ladder. The pilot in Rough 4 flew them back to the cold sea. As they got there, a submarine opened a hatch on its top. The Rough 4 pilot lowered the ladder. Tiblo and Martino dropped themselves into the hatch. Then it closed. The submarine swam back to the base's hangar pool.

As soon as they returned to base, Martino fell asleep from the cold again. Tiblo carried him as he climbed out of the submarine. He took him to a room with bathing columns. He took off Martino's clothes and went down to his bare body with the sponge-like fiber undershorts with a urinal tube and container, taped to the left trunk. Tiblo grabbed a ladder and an oxygen-breathing mask, which he put on Martino's face. Tiblo climbed up the ladder and carefully placed Martino in the bathing column. As soon as the column filled up completely with water, Tiblo turned on a switch that created warm head bubbles rising from the vent at the base of the column. Other militias and the freedom fighters entered the room.

"Well, if it isn't Master Izodorro," said a robot in the back of the crowd, known as the Invisi-Bot, the human-like robot who turns invisible in case of danger. He is the helper of the freedom fighters. Skinamar had put an upgrade in him to make him untouchable back on Earth when Zinger told stories to Martino and him.

A robot floated by with a piston needle shot with a special medicine for Martino to stay awake. It pierced into a slot on the cylinder wall of the bathing column. It then pierced into Martino's thigh. All of a sudden, he awoke opening his eyes.

"Survival of this specimen is complete," said the robot.

And so, after Martino's cold cure, he was pulled out of the bathing column and dressed in an orange outfit used as astronaut bed clothing. He sat on a nearby solid rubber bench.

"Master Martino, sir, it's good to see you again," said the Invisi-Bot as he approached Martino.

"Welcome back, buddy!" said Skinamar as he came by and sat next to him on the bench.

"Friends indeed," said Tiblo as he stood a few feet away. He turned to Manda and said, "Thanks to you who got the truth online."

"I had nothing to do with it," said Manda who stood away by the side.

"Well," said Tiblo, "I don't want to push this, but you should keep the blame under your tail."

"Why, you stupid-headed . . ." Manda started to complain to Tiblo, ". . . perverting . . . fur factory!"

Tiblo made a suspicious facial expression as he faced Manda.

"Who's perverting whom?" he asked.

There was no answer. Tiblo walked back to the hangar to check on the Great Red Shark. Martino got off the bench he sat on and followed him down the hallway. As Tiblo worked on the ship regenerating its power, Martino walked by. Tiblo used a sparking drill on metal surfaces around the ship, wearing a mask to prevent bright sparks of light from blinding him. Martino made his thought and said, "I could have killed those monsters completely."

Tiblo looked down at him and said, "And even if you did, those thumblers would have killed you back." He knew about thumblers because of some research of enemy monsters.

"Just because you spoil everything!" Martino complained. "You're a tiger and I'm a human. And my name's Martino Izodorro, not Martin Izodorf; and I'm sick of it."

"Well, the odds are," said Tiblo, "if you want to be part of this federation and on this team, you will need to cooperate on whatever it takes . . . so that you'll help us fight."

"Against whom?"

"Our enemies, the Serpentials."

Martino sighed and decided to take a walk around.

"Captain!" Shana Cargon called from below the Great Red Shark. Tiblo jumped down from the top of the ship and landed on the ground bar below with his paws in front of him as he fell. Then he went to Shana.

"What is it?" he asked.

"These batteries aren't going in right," Shana said as she kept testing the batteries' positions that didn't work.

"Oh, no no no no!" Tiblo shouted running to her. He showed where the batteries were to be. "This one goes there . . ." he pointed to the battery marked A and the slot marked A. ". . . and that one goes here . . ." he pointed to the battery marked B and the slot marked with the same letter. ". . . alright?"

Shana followed the instruction of the matching letters on the batteries and in the slots. They fitted perfectly.

"Thanks a lot," Shana said.

As Tiblo climbed up the escalator on board the Great Red Shark, the human medical scientist Regulto Beauxon approached him, holding a box with the medicine he invented for his beast form.

"Where can I put my medicine?" asked Regulto.

"In a drawer somewhere in a closet at least," said Tiblo.

Regulto went somewhere to find a closet to store his medicine.

CHAPTER 7

SUB FIGHT

As soon as the Serpentials reached the cold planet, their scale ships were about to hatch open for Serpential submarines. They hovered over the icy, cold sea, preparing for the deployment of marine warfare. Then the Heavenly Federal pilots gathered in a group with the freedom fighters in a meeting room.

"Now everyone, stay calm," Tiblo announced. "You'll all have plenty of time to fight these subs until they intrude on us and destroy our base. Back up as many subs as you can while it can take all your strength. Manda, proceed."

Manda continued the announcement, "There will be two pilots in each ship, one for driving, and the other for shooting. Our submarines contain autopilots for any emergency of drowning pilots out of ships."

"Two pilots against a giant scale ship?" asked a male canine pilot.

"That's bogus," said a male feline pilot.

Meanwhile, the Serpential subs were deployed into the sea. Contacts were being made online.

"This is Captain Kerbano Kassow," said a cassowary that is the Serpential force captain. "I'll hold off the enemy by a few turns." The Serpential submarines' targeting computers were activated by pirate knights driving them.

The freedom fighters entered their ships in the Water Base's hangar bay. The door underwater opened.

"My Tiger Shark is ready," said Tiblo. "Check your systems, scouts."

"Clover Bird says 'all systems go'," said Martino.

"Wallaby Wing ready to kick serpent tail," said Shana.

"Ape Smacker all set," said Skinamar, "and I'm ready to rip."

"Marine Wolf fine enough and sturdy," said Manda.

"Golden Triceros is set," said Regulto. "I hope I'm brave enough."

"Then prove it!" growled a voice that came from the reflected Rufus the Beast on his windshield. All of the freedom fighters headed out.

Admiral Marwick MacFnurd had built a cassowary-shaped robot that he controlled to block any escape. He shot cannons that were the robots wings spread out to each side. Darth Waternoose's hologram appeared in the communicator on the dashboard.

"Yes, Lord Waternoose," said the admiral. "I'm about to deactivate the shield." He drove his robot by a Heavenly Federal ship on the water with a shield bunker next to it.

As the H.F. pilots fired at the ichthyosaur-like Serpential subs, the lasers reflected off the thick, solid metal armor.

"That armor is too strong for lasers," said Martino. "Use torpedoes wisely." He told the pilots.

"Thank you, comrade," said a male canine pilot through the communication system connected to all microphones on every pilot.

"Relax, Pax," said that same pilot to his partner with the gun. That partner is a male feline named, Paxton, whose name is shortened to "Pax".

"Fire the harpoon," said the canine pilot.

"Gotcha," said the feline. He launched a harpoon with a black plunger-like end on the back of an enemy sub. They flew their ship around and around vertically around to tie the harpoon string on the sub like a yo-yo. The sub spun. The pirate knights inside it were trembling on the floor, walls, and ceiling. The feline pilot reeled the harpoon back in its gun. The submarine spun the other direction as the harpoon reeled in. Other pilots came and shot torpedoes at the sub. It broke into many major pieces. Pirate knights swam out of the explosion and teleported themselves with their communicators.

"Good show, Rough 4," said another pilot. Many other subs shot cannon lasers at other H.F. ships. Tiblo headed for the base's shield bunker. He contacted General Grizzle.

"General," he said. "There is a robot heading to deactivate the shield bunker!"

"Then I better start the evacuation," said the general. He activated the alarm throughout the base. It rang as loud repeatedly.

"Attention, comrades!" the general shouted through a loudspeaker microphone. "The shield is about to be deactivated, so leave as soon as you can in the escape submarines that come in the hangar bay! Be there before the base is destroyed!" He ran to the main office to contact the Heavenly Federal sergeant, Ban Van Dunn, a female fox-type canine.

"Sergeant," the general called. The sergeant went toward the general.

"Yes, sir," she said.

"Go and find out who's controlling that robot," the general commanded.

The sergeant ran to the hangar and waited for a submarine. The general suddenly had a message beep on his communicator. He answered it. It was the Heavenly Federal Admiral, Wanko Wolfgang, a male canine with a right bionic eye.

"General!" he said. "You must get out of there as fast as you can!"

"Don't worry, I will!" said the general. "General Grizzle out!" He quickly turned off his communicator and ran to the hangar for an escape pod, while Sergeant Van Dunn got on a sub to swim up to where the bunker was next to a boat owned by Admiral Wolfgang. Admiral Marwick MacFnurd finally destroyed the bunker. The Sergeant went up to the admiral's robot.

CHAPTER 8

THE SERGEANT'S CAPTURE

Very soon, Tiblo followed the robot by the giant boat. The escape pod with General Grizzle floated up to the surface. The sergeant made it up to the surface in the sub and into the robot by a side hatch. She looked around as she got inside. She found the Serpential admiral in his cockpit.

"You!" she shouted.

"Ah, a Heavenly Federal soldier entering my plot," said the admiral.

"I'm Sergeant Van Dunn," said the sergeant. "I have a warrant for your arrest."

"I'm immune to arrest like every Serpential," said the admiral.

Suddenly, Carpoon appeared from behind and shot a whipping cord that coiled around the sergeant's body and tied her. She struggled to break free.

"I'm Carpoon," he introduced himself, "shell-less turtle bounty hunter. I'm here to find your federation's freedom fighters."

"I haven't seen them," said the sergeant. "They're out in war."

"I see," said Carpoon.

"Not to mention," said the admiral, "we don't need enemies as . . . SLY FEMALE MILITIAS! Gag her!" He commanded Carpoon.

"As you wish," he said. He placed a rubber gag over the sergeant's mouth, tying it behind her head. The he dragged her into a giant can-like hostage container. He left its top door open for a rescuer's trap.

As soon as Tiblo stopped his Tiger Shark ship, he called the other freedom fighters.

"Scouts," he said. The others responded.

"Yes, Captain?" they all said.

"Go back to our base and drive the Great Red Shark out of there!" Tiblo commanded. The freedom fighters went straight back to the base to fly the Great Red Shark out. They parked their ships in the Shark's basement hangar. Skinamar ran up to the head cockpit and started to take off. He flew the ship up through a hatch with a force bubble on the ceiling. The freedom fighters finally left the base before the destruction. The pirate knights were about to destroy the base after everyone's evacuation.

Tiblo jumped out of the Tiger Shark and into the same hatch the sergeant found on top of the robot and fell through that hatch. He heard a rapid humming sound from the sergeant with a gag in her mouth in the hostage container. Tiblo went to her. He untied the gag and took it out of her mouth and tore the whipcord from around her body.

"Look out!" shouted the sergeant. "It's a trap!" Carpoon quickly closed the container's door and locked it by its wheel before anyone could escape. He rolled it out of a floor hatch as it was hooked on a hooking chain. As Admiral MacFnurd started to fly the robot in the air, the hostage container fell into the water. Inside the container, Tiblo took the sergeant and held her close to him pressing his boots and front paws against the cylinder wall of the container.

"What are you trying to do?!" asked the sergeant.

"Just stay with me," said Tiblo. Suddenly, small hatches at the bottom released an enormous amount of white smoke.

"That smoke must be toxic!" exclaimed the sergeant.

"I'll get us out of here!" said Tiblo, grabbing his laser pocket knife from his pack. He lit the knife and stabbed a hole in the top. Water came pouring in from the sea. "Awe, great!" Tiblo said.

Admiral MacFnurd flew the robot into the sky and six yards of the chain hovered and lifted the container out of the sea. Water stopped pouring inside. Tiblo cut a large hole in the lid and he and the sergeant escaped out of the container. They were stranded on the surface of the cold sea. The freedom fighters witnessed them from the Great Red Shark's windshield. Skinamar flew the Shark down to where Tiblo and Sergeant Van Dunn floated. The Shark's basement hangar lowered at the sea's surface and Tiblo and the sergeant swam and grabbed onto the hangar's ledge. They climbed aboard. Skinamar flew the Shark to Admiral Wolfgang's boat, so the freedom fighters would drop off the sergeant. As they got there, General Grizzle climbed out of his escape pod and climbed the side ladder up to the boat's deck. As Skinamar landed the Shark next to the boat, the sergeant jumped to the deck aboard the boat where the rest of the Heavenly Federal forces found shelter. Plenty of ships were landed on its deck.

And so, Tiblo ran up to the Great Red Shark's cockpit, taking his turn to drive it as Skinamar moved away.

CHAPTER 9

EVACUATION RESTRICTION

They were about to leave the cold planet as enemy subs destroyed the base. But all of a sudden, Admiral MacFnurd controlled his robot and moved it in front of the Great Red Shark.

"Your evacuation is restricted!" he said to the freedom fighters. He started to arm his robot's missile-launching wings. "It's time to try our new weapon." He launched multiple missiles out of three holes in each wing.

Skinamar flew his Ape Smacker ship out of the Great Red Shark's basement hangar. He shot the plasma lasers at the robot's body.

"COCKY LITTLE CREATURE!" the admiral shouted.

"Keep holding him, Skinamar!" said Tiblo through the speaker of the helmet microphone by Skinamar's mouth.

Skinamar kept firing. The admiral flew toward the Great Red Shark.

"I'm coming for you!" he said.

Manda suddenly ran down to the hangar to get her Marine Wolf ship as Skinamar held the robot off. She flew out and shot a few twin lasers. She held down the button to lock the target on the robot. As it finished charging, Manda launched a laser orb that homed right at the robot. It shed electrical power.

"URRRRR-AAAAUUUUUGGGHHH!" the admiral screamed. The robot exploded. Its head flew across the sky. It landed on a nearby snowy plain. The admiral climbed out of the wreckage. He set foot on the snow. He used his communicator to teleport himself back to the scale carrier. The freedom fighters headed for space.

"We're heading out!" said Tiblo. "Report in."

"I thought we were goners again," said Shana.

"Awesome shooting, Manda," said Skinamar. "Where did you learn to do that?"

"I saw different ships charge laser shots," said Manda, "so I tried by holding down the fire button." So she and Skinamar flew back aboard the Great Red Shark. Tiblo flew the ship away.

Meanwhile, as Admiral MacFnurd was teleported back with the other Serpentials, he explained. "I've failed to hold them hostage," he said. "They have automatically escaped."

"I've failed too," said Captain Kerbano Kassow (another cassowary). "My traps wouldn't work. I must apologize to Lord Waternoose." He walked to the back of the deck to search for Darth Waternoose.

"We'll need a clever specialist to find those wide-eyed wanderers," said General Fang.

Meanwhile, in the Palace of Sharp, the emperor had a confession. The twin vulture viceroys, Hooker and Blunt Volton joined in the throne room to listen.

"Those wide-eyed wandering enemies of ours will no longer stand a chance," said the emperor.

"We'll need a special somebody to take care of them," said Hooker.

"Our count, with his nobility, shall take an ultimate chance," said the emperor.

The emperor's hand man, Rhomp Fang (the Serpential general's brother, a monáchi with two arms), walked by the throne.

"Our count has arrived," he said.

"Excellent," said the emperor. He pressed a button on the arm of his throne. "Bring in Lord Waternoose," he said through the microphone.

Back on the scale carrier, the Serpential captain made his apology to Darth Waternoose. After that, Waternoose used his force choke on the captain's neck. The captain fell to the floor, hoping to get some air as soon as Waternoose stopped choking him.

"Apology accepted," said Waternoose, "Captain Kassow." The captain barely arose from the floor. Waternoose walked away. A couple of trooper lizards grabbed the captain.

Meanwhile, Commander Karbono Kassow (another cassowary) walked to Waternoose and said, "You have a message from the emperor, my lord."

"I'll see him," said Waternoose. He went into a chamber with a computer table that held up Emperor Sharp's hologram, waiting to speak with Waternoose. He folded his six jointed legs under his bottom, allowing himself to kneel to the floor.

"What is your will, my headmaster?" he asked.

"We have a new plan," said the emperor. "We can put the Death Scale back together, using the power of what can hold it, known as Gem Scales." He hissed as kept explaining. "They shall hold it together again after the Death Scale has been destroyed."

"Our enemies will handle this job, accordingly," said Waternoose, using his top left eye, which sought the future.

"Indeed correct," said the emperor. "Search your feelings, Lord Waternoose." Then his hologram vanished. Waternoose exited the room.

CHAPTER 10

THE SECRET OF THE GEM SCALES

And so, as the freedom fighters flew through space, things were about to come into their minds very soon.

"By the way, Shana," said Tiblo as he remembered the bad start back in the base. "You get five demerits for that emotional complaint about excrements."

"Oy!" said Shana. "I hate demerits!

"Worry not," said Skinamar. "I'm impervious to demerits. No one can outrank me."

"Hey!" Martino called from under a seat. "I found a message plate!" He brought a watch-like disk forward to the rest of the crew. Tiblo grabbed it from Martino's open hand then he opened his paw flat with the disk on it. He turned it on by the small knob on the side. A hologram suddenly appeared. It was a dragon dressed in a pirate knight's armor suit.

"Greetings, fine friends of the Heaven Federation," said the dragon. "My name is Dermazzo Joustiáño. I am count of the Sharp Empire. I give you this message for that your task is to seek these Gem Scales . . ." The hologram switched to five floating gems. ". . . The Serpentials and I have already recovered the first two for the Death Scale's top half. So you must find the remaining three gems and place them in wherever they go in a secret place that fits for each one within each quarter of the biosphere." The hologram switched back to the dragon. "Good luck, freedom fighters. I will see you on the first planet from the Death Scale." The hologram disappeared. Tiblo set the message plate on the dashboard.

"Alright!" he said. "We have a job to do. I'm gonna split the team. Marty, Skinamar, you guys stick around space and make sure Zinger is with you. The rest come with me to that station ahead. I've gotta figure out the case of this." He pointed to a space station outside the windshield.

"Well, I haven't seen Zinger around here," said Martino.

"I'm hiding in here!" a voice called from a nearby closet by the left seat aisle. It was Zinger, the old wasp. He fluttered his wings and hovered toward Martino.

"Zinger," said Martino. "Glad to see you again."

"I heard you're all on a quest to put the Death Scale's artifacts in place," said Zinger. "Those gem scales are to hold the Death Scale together."

"Right," said Skinamar as he hopped by Martino in his seat. "Marty and I are buddies."

"Come with me," said Zinger. He led Martino and Skinamar down to the Great Red Shark's basement hangar. Martino jumped into the Clover Bird as Skinamar jumped into the Ape Smacker. Zinger had a floating pod-like transport of his own that would follow the other two. They flew out of the hangar. When they were gone, Tiblo and the rest of the crew flew to the station ahead.

Remembering the top half of the Death Scale put together, Martino, Skinamar, and Zinger found the southeastern quarter to the right of their sight in space. They flew to it. As they got there, they landed their ships next to the mountain of dry ice placed in the east desert of the Death Scale. In front of the mountain was a dam that replaced carbon dioxide with nitrogen, forming the Nitro River. The mountain of dry ice was called, Chart Gooney.

"There's the Nitro River," said Skinamar as the heroes leaped out of their ships, "just like I remember it when we first got on this biosphere."

"There's the entrance," said Zinger as he spotted a cave mouth on the mountainside nearby. The three travelers walked to it. Inside the cave were walls and columns of dry ice. Skinamar felt a chill.

"I'm cold," he said. "Are *you*, Marty?"

"Not really," said Martino.

"It's easy to get lost in here," said Zinger.

Skinamar looked around, chattering his teeth. He felt some dry ice on a nearby mound of an ice fence. He figured how cold it was and suddenly felt a burning sting.

"AH EE OOH AUGH!" Skinamar jumped and screamed.

"Skinamar!" said Martino. "Two things, okay?" He held two fingers up. "Be quiet . . ." He rested his other hand's finger on one of the fingers he held up. ". . . and stop goofing around." He put his finger on the other finger held up. "Now go over there and see if you can find a secret teleporter." He pointed at the path in front of Skinamar by the right of their position.

"Teleporter??" said Skinamar as he looked at the path Martino pointed to. He turned his head to Martino and said, "I thought we were looking for the gem scale."

"We *are* looking for the gem scale," said Martino. "It should be in a secret place hidden in this cave and it should have a teleporter."

"What makes you think about that?" asked Skinamar.

"It's in a bunch of stories I heard in school," said Martino as he went straight and walked that path.

"May Artidector be with us," said Zinger.

"Yeah," said Skinamar. "He's walking that way . . ." He pointed to the path Martino walked. ". . . and I'm going this way." He walked the path to the right. Zinger stayed in the same place.

As Skinamar walked his path, there were stalactites and stalagmites of crystal clear glitter and dry ice shedding steam. Suddenly, he witnessed a stone pedestal with gold light.

"What do you know?" said Skinamar. "That was easy for Marty to say." He scurried to that pedestal ahead. He admitted that it was a teleporter.

Meanwhile, Martino found a room with no way in on the end of the path he walked.

"Wow," he said. "At least we might know where the gem scale is. But how do I get in there?" There was wide clear window in front of him. Behind it was a matching teleporter like the one Skinamar found, and there happened to be a column of with the gem scale frozen inside. The gem scale was colored yellow.

CHAPTER 11

TIBLO'S DESTINATION

Back in space, Tiblo and the rest of the crew flew into the space station ahead. They landed in the hangar bay at the bottom. As they landed, Tiblo had a decision to make.

"Now everyone, stay in the ship until I get back!" he commanded. "I've got places to seek on research." He walked off the ship as the others obediently remained on.

Tiblo walked through the halls up to an upper floor of the station. On the next floor was a room of research computers. Tiblo found the Heavenly Federal lieutenant, Mavis Wuka, a female feline with a bionic right hand with three appending fingers replacing her paw that was cut off once by a pirate knight in battle. She worked on a computer as Tiblo approached her.

"Hey, Lieutenant," he said, "I'm looking for a map system for the Death Scale."

"Go in that room," said the lieutenant, pointing to a square doorway halfway down the room, "and find Jer the tapir and Professor Fester Whiskey."

"Thank you," said Tiblo. He walked to the room where the lieutenant showed him.

In that room, there was a tapir teaching a class of young students for the Heaven Federation, and a fat cat scientist testing unidentified chemicals. The tapir wearing a brown and yellow cap was Jer. The fat cat in a large white coat was Professor Fester Whiskey.

"Jer!" Tiblo called in, entering the room and interrupting the tapir's training lesson.

The tapir turned to Tiblo and said, "Captain Tigro! It's been a while since we met, what are you doing here?"

"I need a graphic map for the Death Scale's current appearance," said Tiblo.

"Oh yes," said Jer. "I'll get the professor. Kids, wait for me in here and do something free as you wait." The students followed his instruction and did research on a nearby computer. Tiblo and Jer went to the professor working with robots by a conveyor belt.

"Professor Whiskey," said Jer, "Captain Tigro wants to see a map of the Death Scale."

"Ah yes," said the professor. "My old master must have left a graphic map globe in here." He went to a nearby cabinet and opened a top drawer by unhooking a connection by the handle. He snatched a small globe with a tiny light under a lens. He brought it back by Tiblo. The professor pressed a side button. The light shone through the lens and showed a holographic map of the Death

Scale; the top hemisphere was together, but the bottom quarters were still far apart. The only thing missing was the Horrendo Sea, which belongs on the back of the Death Scale.

"The sea on this has vanished in the distance," said Professor Whiskey. "It's up to you and your scouts to find it in a rock."

"Well, I thought it was still there," said Tiblo pointing to the empty hole on the Death Scale's posterior hemisphere where the sea was, "but it doesn't seem to exist anymore."

"It should be in a farther reach of space," said the professor. "Quite far."

"Even further than you realize, Captain," said Jer.

"Then I suppose it should be here," said Tiblo showing two fingers pinching air far behind the hologram. "Thanks. That's all I need to know."

"Good luck, Captain," said the professor.

"We'll meet again some other time," said Jer.

Tiblo left the room and walked back to the hangar. He climbed back aboard the Great Red Shark where the others waited for him.

"There is a sea on the Death Scale that is missing," said Tiblo. "We're going to find it." He started the Great Red Shark and it hovered above the floor and flew out of the space station. Into space they went; they searched for the Horrendo Sea far behind the Death Scale.

CHAPTER 12

THE FIRST GEM SCALE

And so, back with Martino and Skinamar in Chart Gooney, Skinamar was teleported to the secret room where Martino found the gem scale frozen in the column through the clear window. Martino saw Skinamar appearing from the teleporter and saw the gem scale. He suddenly found Martino through the window.

"Marty!" he shouted. "The teleporter is at the path I took from back there!"

"I'll be there!" Martino said through the window. He ran back the path he walked and went back to the junction and followed Skinamar's footsteps all the way to the teleporter. Suddenly, as Skinamar waited for Martino, a henchmonster appeared. It was a crutch with a funny face on the middle cushion bar.

"Who disturbs my slumber?!" the crutch bellowed. "I'm Babba the Crutch. I am authorized to keep that gem scale guarded in that ice column if anyone comes to get it."

"I'm Skinamarinky-Dinky-Dink Skinamarinky-Doo," said Skinamar.

"Are you willing to face me?" asked Babba the Crutch.

"I'm waiting for my friend, Marty," said Skinamar. Martino suddenly appeared as soon as he heard the conversation.

"Martino Izodorro," he said, "at your service."

"Ah, a human and an orangutan," said Babba the Crutch. "Ready to fight?"

Martino grabbed his disk launchers out of his backpack and aimed them at Babba.

"I've got a surprise," Babba said. He hurled out a yellow bomb with a smiley face.

"Oh, look!" said Skinamar. "A yellow happy face . . . BOMB?!?" He was shocked as the fuse lit itself on fire. He quickly slapped the bomb towards the ice column with the gem scale. The bomb's fuse shortened, and then it exploded. The column shattered to pieces but the gem scale remained in one piece.

"Nooo!" shouted Babba. "The gem scale is loose!" He hopped to the gem scale on his tan rubber foot. "You infidels have outsmarted me!"

"We'll see about that!" said Martino. He shot his disk launchers at Babba repeatedly as Babba jumped and hopped to avoid the shots. Until at last, a disk shot hit him and Babba smoked and fell apart on the ground.

"Yes! We did it!" shouted Skinamar.

"Our first gem scale is in need," said Martino. He went forward to the gem scale to pick it up. Before he could, Artidector appeared.

"Excellent work, Martino," he said. "Now this gem scale is free; it shall go to its slot hidden in the dry ice mines by the Death Scale's south pole."

Martino was about to grab the gem scale.

"Touch it not!" Artidector told him. "It is a special type of artifact. Spread your hands around it and it will hover in front of you."

Martino followed his instruction, when he set his hands a few inches off the sides of the gem scale, a magic force from his imagination caused the scale to hover as he lifted his arms off the ground. The scale hovered and landed in his backpack.

"Let's get out of here," said Martino. Artidector disappeared. Martino and Skinamar exited the room through the same teleporter they used. They went back to the junction where Zinger waited for them. Zinger perched on the fence by the junction. He chilled a bit as he sat on it. Suddenly, Martino and Skinamar showed up.

"We have the gem scale," said Martino.

"Great work, boys," said Zinger. "Now let's leave this mountain and get it back to its slot in the dry ice mines." He hovered into the air and led Martino and Skinamar out of Chart Gooney's cavern. As they left, Babba the Crutch's pieces lifted from the ground and he began to fix himself.

CHAPTER 13

THE HORRENDO SEA

And so, Tiblo with Shana, Manda, Regulto, and the Invisi-Bot, found the Horrendo Sea floating in a rock bowl in space.

"This is the lost sea from the Death Scale," said Tiblo. He flew the Great Red Shark into the sea. He dove with it into the water. There were strange kinds of sea monsters living in it. At the bottom and middle of its abyss was a palace. As Tiblo landed on the seafloor, sand floated from the floor and hovered throughout the open water. Behind the Shark was a cave filled with mostly seaweed. At the foot of the slope ahead was the Horrendo Palace. It appeared in a crater that formed the deepest part of the sea.

"Quite a smooth landing here," said Tiblo.

"If my calculations are correct," said the Invisi-Bot as he studied the sea, "we should find the gem scale in that palace down there. The creatures here are giraffe fish, crocodile fish, dragon dolphins, torpedo sharks, and decopuses. The decopuses form a navy in that palace down there. Their ruler is called the Water Queen." According to his research, giraffe fish were large giraffe-shaped fish, crocodile fish were fish shaped like crocodiles, dragon dolphins were fancy colored dolphins with webbed fins and thorns running down their spines, torpedo sharks were slim sharks that could swim fast, and decopuses were like octopuses with ten tentacles instead of eight.

"These creatures can still be dangerous," said Regulto looking out a window.

Suddenly, a gold sand giraffe fish swam out of the cave behind. Its neck was ten feet long. Its head was shaped like a real giraffe with gnawing teeth for cutting seaweed for food. This fish bumped at the Great Red Shark's tailfin with engines. Two crocodile fish appeared from the cave. One was pink with a sail on its back and the other was blue-green with spinal plates. Their heads were shaped like real crocodiles. Tiblo saw the fish from the back window.

"I'm going to that cave," he said. "I won't let these fish tear this ship apart." He ran to a nearby closet to get some scuba gear.

"I'm coming with you," said Manda, following him at the closet. She also grabbed scuba gear.

As Tiblo grabbed his gear out of the closet, he went down to the lower deck to change. Then so did Manda after she waited a few minutes. As Tiblo finished changing into a diving suit, he ran back up to the upper deck to give instructions.

"Regulto," he said to Regulto at the dashboard, "stay with the Invisi-Bot and watch over the ship. If anything comes, use one of the machine guns over there." He pointed to the middle of the ship's body with the ladders at the side. Then Tiblo went to Shana in the back of the deck behind the seats.

"Shana," he said. "Go down in your Wallaby Wing and check out the palace."

"Piece of cake," said Shana. She hopped down to the under deck. When she got there, the whole deck was flooded by the water from the sea intruding. She climbed aboard her Wallaby Wing ship and the doors opened, allowing even more water in the basement hangar.

"This is Shana," she said through her wrist communicator. "We're being flooded. Out." She turned it off.

Tiblo and Manda put on the scuba gear as they walked down to the flooded deck. They wore helmets of solid plastic like astronauts. The breathing machines ran from their mouths into tanks of oxygen on their backs. They swam out of the deck and around the giant fishes swimming by. They headed for the cave. As they swam there, Manda remembered the beautiful things she saw on her home planet when the emperor bound and gagged her and her sister as that sister drowned but Manda was saved by Artidector. She noticed sparkling gold and silver coral and seaweed. Suddenly, there was a shark swimming in circles around the cave. It was mostly colored black. It was a torpedo shark. Tiblo and Manda set their paddle boots on the cave's floor.

"The floor sure feels soft," said Manda. "It feels like mud."

"It *is* mud," said Tiblo. "There are a lot of soils mixed here underwater." "That algae sucker is definitely alien," he said as he noticed a three-eye stalked algae eater on the ceiling.

"I have an awful feeling about this," said Manda. She and Tiblo kept breathing their supply of oxygen when suddenly, the torpedo shark swam toward them at rocket speed.

"Watch OUT!" Tiblo shouted, grabbing Manda's tail pulling her towards him. Suddenly, a gray humpbacked giraffe fish woke up and ate some sparkling seaweed.

"I should research these beasts when I get home," said Tiblo. He and Manda quickly swam out of the cave before the shark could get back to them. They swam back to the Great Red Shark. A crocodile fish swam by and Regulto shot it with one of the machine guns under the ladders. The fish roared in agony.

Meanwhile, Shana was still looking around the Horrendo Palace, steering her ship and searching for a hidden entrance. She went below and finally found the secret entrance on the first floor, a rectangular tunnel with a pressure of air at the other end inside. She started to go back to the Great Red Shark.

CHAPTER 14

THE DRY ICE MINES

Martino and Skinamar walked to the polar cap of dry ice down the desert from Chart Gooney with Zinger fluttering with them.

"We must find the enemy mine," said Zinger. "It is in there somewhere."

"There's no entrance," said Martino.

"There will be made by me," said Skinamar. He pulled his sunray phaser out of his backpack. He shot a hole in a wall of dry ice. An orange beam melted the ice. "Now we can go in," he said.

So the three heroes entered the hole. Inside was a cavern full of a maze. It was dark and some dry ice was sparkling. Martino led the way straight, then left, then right, until suddenly, there was a real mine with carts on railroads. Nobody appeared in the mine.

"Check out these carts," said Skinamar. "I'll bet one of them leads to where the gem scale goes."

"I don't think so, Skinamar," said Martino.

"The secret is to follow those roads wherever they lead," said Skinamar. He jumped in a nearby mine cart. "Come on, guys."

"Alright," said Martino, climbing aboard. Zinger fluttered his wings behind and perched on the side edge between Martino and Skinamar. Skinamar pushed the front end wall with his belly repeatedly. He inhaled much air and inflated himself like a balloon. He exhaled the air rapidly to the back of the cart to make it go. The cart rolled and began to speed up down its railroad. It rolled downhill straight ahead on its path, and then it hit the floor at the foot of the slope. It rolled over an empty air space. The cart rounded a corner and stopped at a dead end in a next cave. The heroes jumped out of the cart. They followed a nearby tunnel that even took them deeper into the mine. It was until they found a cubic stone with a crater on one side facing up.

"I wonder if the gem scale fits here," said Martino. He took the gem scale out of his backpack, but without touching it, it hovered up to his grasping hand. He surrounded the scale with his hands and set it in the crater. It fitted perfectly.

"Yes!" shouted Skinamar. "We did it!" The gem scale glowed and shone as bright as a distant star. It began to move the piece of the Death Scale back to its original position. It took a while. Martino, Skinamar, and Zinger were automatically teleported back to the mine's entrance by flying sparks of magic surrounding them. They were in the same place Skinamar shot for the entrance. They went out of it and walked back to where their ships were landed by Chart Gooney. As they got there, Artidector appeared.

"Excellent work," he said. "The Death Scale's gem scales are to put it back together. If you stay here, you will be caught by the biosphere's inhabitants."

"We're trying to get on our ships," said Martino. "We need to find our friends in their quest."

"That's not quite a good idea, Marty," said Zinger. "Otherwise we would be caught on their location, too."

Martino was about to jump into his Clover Bird ship.

"Martino," said Artidector. "I not want to lose you to the Serpentials the way I lost Nala Boomer."

"Neither do I," said Zinger.

"You won't," said Martino. He climbed into his ship's cockpit.

"Good form, Marty," said Skinamar jumping into the cockpit of his Ape Smacker ship.

"When I was a mortal," said Artidector, "over a thousand years ago, I saw my children wander the skies as medieval knights fought in their battles. I thought they were still on my side, but now today I have found my two eldest sons. They are taking care of the princess floating in space while I find my other children."

Zinger flew into his space pod.

"We better go," said Martino. "We're wasting time."

"Martino," Artidector got his attention. "Resist not to the Sharp Empire's schemes." He raised one of his taloned gray hands. "That leads to the Serpent's Ghost."

"The Serpent's Ghost?" Martino asked.

"It is the soul of Lucifer shed from his death that helped create the Sharp Empire," Artidector explained.

"Thanks a lot, O Arty," said Skinamar.

"Good luck," said Artidector.

"Let's go," said Martino. He and Skinamar closed their cockpits with their ships' cover shields. They lifted off. Zinger closed his space pod and made it hover out into space, following the others. Artidector vanished and continued his quest for the rest of his children.

CHAPTER 15

THE WATER QUEEN

And so, Tiblo with the rest of the crew waited for Shana round the Horrendo Palace.

"I found the secret entrance," she said through her communicator.

"We're coming," said Tiblo calling her back.

The palace's entrance for craft was hidden at the bottom as a rectangular prism tunnel. Tiblo, Manda, and Regulto went down to the flooded basement hangar and swam to their ships. They jumped into the cockpits. They flew out and followed Shana to the nearby palace. The Invisi-Bot stayed in the Great Red Shark and took over the pilot's cockpit.

"Time to run this ship around these fish," he said. He used the acceleration pedal and used the steering handle to move the ship around and avoided the giant fish swimming about.

"Oh, where is Skinamar when I need him?" the Invisi-Bot asked himself. He pressed the invisibility button on his chest and made himself invisible as a ghost. "That's more like it," he said.

And so, the freedom fighters went through the secret entrance at the palace's basement. The monsters living in the palace were known as decopuses, squid-like creatures with octopus-like heads, ten electrical tentacles, and three eyes. The defenders had two tentacles with boosters, and the attackers were fierce fighters excellent with their tentacles. The defenders floated with neutral buoyancy outside the palace. Attackers were kept in water-filled areas within it.

The freedom fighters entered the tunnel and found the surface of water affected by air pressure up to the blue hallways of the palace. They climbed with their ships up to the surface. They jumped out and grabbed the edge of the square pressure pool. They climbed up to the tile floor. Tiblo suddenly had a decision to make.

"You three stick around," he said to the others. "I'm going down this way to check things out." He pointed at a nearby hallway and walked down it. Shana found another hallway at the other side of the room.

"I'll bet there's more evidence that way," she said as she pointed her front paw that direction of the hallway she saw.

"No fat chances, Shana," said Manda.

"It's a good thing I have my alter ego medicine," said Regulto as he lifted a small cylinder flask of his medicine in his trousers' left thigh pocket. So he and Manda followed Shana, who hopped down the hallway.

Meanwhile, as Tiblo dashed the rest of the other hallway and braked for stop, he witnessed a laboratory of aquaria containing earthly and even alien kinds of marine species.

"This place is pathetically conspicuous," he said. The specimen swam around their tanks. Tiblo found a control panel at the other side of the room from where he was. He ran to it. There were many different colored buttons and a long lever with an orange bulb. He typed various buttons and the tanks' wind vents were activated, then the filters and so was an occurrence of mutation in the creatures. They turned into hideous monsters, such as angler fish with different numbers of eyes, sturgeons with bulb-top antennae, or eels with razor-sharp teeth. An alarm rang out loud through the halls. Tiblo quickly pulled the orange bulb lever that opened the large metal door that led to the next room. He ran to it.

Meanwhile in a far away room with a decopus navy, the decopus admiral, Gorkon made contact with the giant decopus guardian known as the Water Queen.

"You have intruders, your majesty!" said the admiral. The Water Queen armed herself with her tentacles folded around her body.

Meanwhile again, Shana led the others through the hallway opposite of where Tiblo went. Shana and Regulto found another control panel like the one that Tiblo found. Shana pressed a key on the panel. It suddenly made weapons strike and fly down the hallway to the left. A defense system was activated.

"This is odd," said Shana. Spears sprung from holes in the ground. Sawing wheels rolled across the floor from one side wall to the other. There was a metal door at the end. The weapons did everything back and forth, blocking the hallway.

"There's the door," said Manda. She pulled the orange bulb lever on the control panel which opened the metal door. She pulled her old dark purple cape out of her pack and folded it into a rectangular wad like a towel and walked down the hallway avoiding the spears ahead one striking up and two down, then the opposing point. She placed her folded cape flat against the left way where a saw wheel rolled to leave its path. The saw came and stopped at the slit where Manda put her folded cape. All of the weapons stopped.

"I thought that cape would get ripped," said Regulto.

"It would if it was straightly stretched across without wrinkles," said Manda. "That's what my mother told me before she died." So she, Shana, and Regulto walked the rest of the hallway to the open doorway, standing aside every frozen weapon. They finally entered the big room.

Meanwhile, Tiblo was confronted by a large block in the room without a ladder. He decided to use his power from Artidector, which was the ability to climb by using his claws. He spread his paws wide and his claws formed like hooks. He slammed one paw on the wall of the block he was next to. Then he slammed his other paw on a higher section of the wall. He started climbing the block about twenty feet off the floor. As soon as he got to the top of the block there was a giant tank that contained the Water Queen. Her crown was gold with square and rhombic jewels and swinging spike balls held at the side tips by chains. Tiblo faced the monster. Suddenly, Shana, Manda, and Regulto arrived at the block that Tiblo was on. Shana hopped on her tail like any kangaroo would do and sprung herself high up in the air to the top of the block. Her high bounce came from Artidector. Manda used a power from Artidector that allowed her to vanish from the floor and teleport up to the top of the block. But Regulto had no way to get up there, so he remained on the floor. Tiblo was staring at an artifact of a glass globe containing a blue thin gem. That was one of the gem scales.

"Aye, Captain!" Shana shouted behind Tiblo. He turned to her and Manda.

"How did you girls get up here?" he asked.

"I hopped on my tail up here," said Shana.

"And I teleported myself," said Manda.

"Where's Regulto?" Tiblo asked.

"He's back on the floor," said Shana.

"These were our powers from Artidector," said Manda.

"Very impressive," said Tiblo. "I'm busy right now, so go back and wait with Regulto." He continued looking at the blue gem scale.

"It doesn't look like you're busy," said Shana. "It looks more like you're staring at something up there." She saw what Tiblo was staring at.

"It's one of those gem scales that we're looking for," said Tiblo. The Water Queen stared face to face with him.

"Wait for me later," he said to Shana and Manda. "I must work alone."

"I knew he'd be harsh," Shana said to Manda.

"Let's get back to Regulto," said Manda. She teleported herself back to the floor where Regulto remained. Shana hopped and fell down there landing on her front paws. Regulto suddenly found a lever next to the giant tank. He ran to it. Suddenly, his beast reflection appeared on the tank's glass wall.

"Leave it alone, Regulto," the beast said.

"I wonder what it does," said Regulto.

"I'm warning you," said the beast. Regulto reached the lever.

"NOOO!" Manda shouted when she saw him.

Regulto curiously pulled the lever. Suddenly, the tank's glass wall lowered down slowly, letting water escape. The Water Queen grew angry as the glass lowered and water emptied out filling the room. Tiblo took out his twin blasters and prepared himself for combat. The flood continued to rise. The entire room was half full of water. The Water Queen started to rage, waving and slamming her tentacles on the water surface. Tiblo fired repeated at the monster. He shot the spike balls on the chains hanging from her crown. The balls exploded. The chains hung loose. Meanwhile, Shana, Manda and Regulto swam in the water. Regulto found his beast reflection on the surface.

"We can do it, Regulto," the beast said.

"What are you talking about?" Regulto asked.

"You know what to do," said the beast. "Your medicine. And together, we must drain this room." Regulto nodded his head, with his mouth half open. He felt afraid.

"I've got to be brave," he said. He grabbed the flask of his medicine out of his trousers' side pocket. He swam to the Water Queen's tank where happened to be a giant throne.

"Regulto!" Manda shouted as she found him. "Where are you going?!"

"It's our only chance!" Regulto called back. He swam over the tank's floor and in the middle was a drain. He drank his medicine grabbing the cork plug out of the mouth and putting it to his lips. He swallowed it. His mouth opened wide, allowing him to yawn but nearly scream. He dove into the water. He took off his suit as he transformed into his alter ego, Rufus the beast. The beast swam down to the drain. He grabbed the handles that opened the slits of the drain. The water in the room lowered its level. The Water Queen shivered and shook. Tiblo fired at her while she was in distraction with her attention of the water draining. As Rufus floated on the water's surface Regulto's reflection appeared in front of him.

"Bravo, Rufus!" he said. "Bravo!"

Tiblo finally defeated the Water Queen. The water level reached to the floor. The tank was empty. The room's water level was about one foot high. Manda and Shana could feel solid ground under the surface. Tiblo jumped from the block he was on back on the floor, landing on his paws and splashing some water. Rufus walked out of the Water Queen's empty tank. The only thing to worry about was the gem scale.

CHAPTER 16

THE SECOND GEM SCALE

The blue gem scale was contained on the ceiling of the Water Queen's tank by a crystal ball attached to an elastic rubber cord. The freedom fighters walked into the tank. Rufus witnessed the gem scale on the ceiling.

"That's what Artidector told us about," he said. He slammed the wall with his fists. It caused the walls and ceiling to quake. The crystal ball swung from side to side. Tiblo quickly shot the elastic cord with one of his blasters. The ball fell nearly twenty feet to the floor. It broke and shattered to pieces. The gem scale remained in one piece.

"He says not to touch it," said Rufus. He merely changed back to Regulto by huffing and puffing. His muscles shrank and his fur vanished. He still had his trousers on. He needed his boots back.

Tiblo went to the gem scale. He put his paws a few inches by the sides. He lifted his arms and the scale followed his movement hovering higher in midair. Suddenly, it slowly hovered toward the Water Queen's giant golden throne. It inserted itself into the throne's head plate. The throne elevated itself with the platform underneath it. It lowered far down into the palace's basement. Just then, Artidector appeared.

"Excellent work, Tiblo," he said. "The Death Scale's firing weapon system will not be operational until it is put completely together again."

"We must leave this place," said Tiblo to the others. So the freedom fighters left the tank then the big room.

"Good luck, freedom fighters," said Artidector. "The force shall be with you."

After a while, the freedom fighters got to their waiting ships floating on the pressured water surface in the basement room's pool. They climbed into the cockpits and activated the ships. They went back through the square prism tunnel and out to the sea's open water. Then they found the Great Red Shark waiting on the seafloor. The freedom fighters flew their ships in the basement hangar and landed them. They jumped out and swam to the staircase up to the top deck where the Invisi-Bot took over the pilot's cockpit.

"We're back," said Tiblo far behind the Invisi-Bot.

"Oh!" said the Invisi-Bot in surprise. "Here you can drive away." He moved away from the driver's seat allowing Tiblo to set himself on it. He grabbed the steering handle bars. He set his back paw on the acceleration pedal.

The Great Red Shark lifted off. It finally left the Horrendo Sea, zooming out of the water.

"We must find Marty, Skinamar, and Zinger," said Tiblo. "They're somewhere out here."

The Horrendo Sea slowly moved back to its fitting puzzle position. A while later the Death Scale was nearly completely put together, but the last gem scale to find had not been located.

And so, Tiblo found the three ships with Martino, Skinamar, and Zinger. The water in the basement hangar was emptied. So they landed in there. The freedom fighters were reunited once again. Tiblo looked at the monitor screen at the side of the dashboard. The green text said:

> Meet us on the planet Geodou, the first planet
> that follows the Death Scale.
>
> —Count Joustiáño

As Tiblo read the message, he located the planet Geodou on a computer type of compass on the dashboard. It was far to the left of the Great Red Shark about 3 million miles away. Following that direction, Tiblo turned the ship left and followed the path ahead. He turned on the hyper drive. The ship zoomed out of sight.

Moments passed. The freedom fighters sitting in the seats of the top deck fell asleep. But Tiblo stayed awake to drive the Great Red Shark. Suddenly, Manda awoke when she felt she had to use a restroom. She stood up out of her seat and spread her legs to release urine in her current diaper. Martino, about two seats to the right, barely opened his eyes and saw Manda, sitting up.

"Manda," said Martino. "Do you need to change your diaper?"

"I-I can't during hyper drive," said Manda. She sat back down in her seat. Martino closed his eyes and went back to sleep.

CHAPTER 17

THE FIGHTING LIZARDS

As soon as an hour passed with the hyper drive, the freedom fighters reached the last mile to planet Geodou. The planets that followed the Death Scale had neither day nor night, because there was no star to determine their current time. So the skies appeared dark with outer space and some nearby planets or moons.

Tiblo was about to land the Great Red Shark on a wide-open part of the planet's surface. As he did, Manda went into the storage closet to change her diaper. The other freedom fighters stepped off the ship on the entrance's conveyor belt. Manda stepped out of the closet dressed in her tunic and trousers. A moment passed as soon as the freedom fighters scrambled across the desert plain. The next four monsters soon to face are "fighting lizards", four dinosaurs with unique looks and fighting skills. Their names were Dreadosaurus, Karatesaurus, Ninjasaurus and Sumosaurus.

Dreadosaurus was a gray-bodied, beige bellied with tail underside, red eyed, clawed, and spine thorn dinosaur with red flexible dreadlocks sticking up in a frill. Karatesaurus was an orange duck-billed, Tsintaosaur-like dinosaur with a dark blue crest and bright green eyes, tip of the crest and nails, and also a yellow belly and tail underside. Ninjasaurus was a purple theropod with bright green eyes, claws, and stegosaur-like spine plates, and a gray belly and tail underside. Sumosaurus was a blue tyrannosaur-like dinosaur with bright red claws, eyes, eye brow horns, and spikes running down his spine; and a bluish green belly and tail underside.

These dinosaurs headed to where the freedom fighters were traveling. Ahead of them far away was a building that went over the edge of a cliff. The fighting lizards suddenly flipped over the heroes and confronted them.

"Going somewhere?" they all asked.

"We're heading for the location to find Count Dermazzo Joustiáño," said Tiblo.

"First you must face us in fight," said Dreadosaurus raising his fists.

"Handle my fighting skills," said Karatesaurus testing his kicks and chops.

"BRAWL!!" roared Sumosaurus.

"Whoa!!" said Skinamar as his head wiggled after that roar. "He's a big one alright."

The fight began. Dreadosaurus would pack a typical punch like a bully or a street thug. Karatesaurus could perform real karate moves. Ninjasaurus could fight like a real ninja. Sumosaurus could wrestle in any sumo wrestler style.

"I'm good at fighting," said Shana. "My father taught me how." She hopped to the dinosaurs and performed a break dancing kick by spinning on her head. Karatesaurus tried a leaping kick but he got knocked away. Shana got up on her feet. Dreadosaurus charged like a ram at Shana and she blocked his head. Her muzzle hovered over the frill of dreadlocks. Dreadosaurus stopped. Shana went to the back and grabbed him by the tail and started to swing him around and around. She swung him so fast until she released him. Dreadosaurus fell to the dirt far away and drove his face into the ground.

After a second the fight continued. Karatesaurus and Ninjasaurus approached and leaped into the air with their claws up from flinging their arms toward the sky. Then they dropped to the ground.

"I'll handle the big guy over there," said Tiblo as he grabbed his blasters and headed for Sumosaurus behind the rest of the dinosaurs.

Ninjasaurus did a jump twist kick around each freedom fighter. As Tiblo faced Sumosaurus, Sumosaurus lifted one foot and stomped to make an earthquake. He swung his arms and tried to smack Tiblo, but he dodged his hands. Tiblo suddenly gave a kung fu kick right at Sumosaurus's chin which knocked him down. Tiblo flipped backward after the kick. Sumosaurus fainted. Shana tried fighting Ninjasaurus, but he knocked her away with a spinning kick with his legs and tail. Shana landed on her back a few yards away from the battle.

Suddenly, Dreadosaurus lifted his face out of the dirt and shook it off. He looked at the fighting scene. Karatesaurus was fighting with Skinamar, and he kept dodging his attacks by jumping and skipping to the sides, avoiding the chops and kicks. Karatesaurus flipped in the air and did a stomp kick after spinning. Skinamar rolled forward to avoid the stomp. Karatesaurus missed him. Skinamar grabbed him by the neck with his stretching arm and threw him to a far away part of the desert over his head.

Meanwhile Dreadosaurus arrived back. Sumosaurus barely got up. Tiblo gave a warning, "Everybody go! This is too dangerous!" The freedom fighters stayed clear of the dinosaurs, but Tiblo stayed within the fight. Karatesaurus returned by skipping back with his brothers. Suddenly, Tiblo began to spread something in his mind. It was fury ability. His head was fed up with it and out it spread with a blast of holographic flames that blasted away the four fighting lizards. The freedom fighters ducked and covered. After a few seconds, the blast disappeared. The freedom fighters awoke.

"Way to go, tiger," said Skinamar as he tried breathing the air again.

Meanwhile, above the atmosphere on that planet was a satellite with a security camera. It focused on the sight of the freedom fighters from over the atmosphere. The camera's view was displayed in a security room.

Count Joustiáño was there with some Serpential officers, watching the camera's view.

"Impressive," said Joustiáño as he remembered how Tiblo ended the fight. "Let us send the troopers to them and . . ." He pointed his finger to the exit door. ". . . invite them to dinner."

"As you wish," said the cassowary officer at the dashboard with the view display. He pressed a button on the communication system on the dashboard to call the scale troopers.

"Troops!" he called. "We have outcasts in the desert. I want you to bring them to us."

"Right away," said one of the troopers through his wrist communicator. He turned it off. The cassowary's hologram vanished. The troopers marched out of a garage by the hangar of the strange building to the desert in search for the freedom fighters.

Meanwhile the freedom fighters started walking toward the strange building far away.

"So, Shana," Martino started a conversation, "where did you learn to fight like that?"

"My father taught me," said Shana, "when I was a little joey, before I was banished. He even taught me how to box."

"That's wonderful," said Skinamar. "And Tiblo, where did you learn that explosive-looking move?"

"It's tiger fury," said Tiblo. "I do it when I can't resist in battle."

"Oh no!" said Regulto. "Someone's coming!" It was the scale troopers. They finally arrived where the freedom fighters stopped walking. The freedom fighters put their hands/paws in the air. The troopers walked behind them and herded them with their guns pointing behind to the building. The walk continued.

CHAPTER 18

THE SERPENTIAL DINNER

As soon as they all got to the building, the freedom fighters were brought forth to the Serpential forces. They were sent to a large restaurant with many tables. General Karchong Fang and other officers grabbed various tables and some of them sat at the longest table in the middle of the place. The general took a seat at it. The freedom fighters sat in different chairs in the middle table, somewhat far apart or close by.

"This reminds me of the Knights of the Round Table," said Skinamar.

"I haven't eaten for days," said Martino.

"Me neither, kid," said Tiblo.

Suddenly, Darth Waternoose arrived in the doorway. Tiblo got up from where he sat and grabbed one of his blasters and tried shooting Waternoose. Waternoose put up his seven-fingered hand to block the shots. He used his magnet force to grab Tiblo's blaster, making it fly to his hand.

"We would be honored if you will join us for dinner," said Waternoose.

Pirate knights and Serpential officers sat with the freedom fighters. Menus appeared as computer lists. Carnivore menus, herbivore menus, and even omnivore menus were on the lists as all the sitters scrolled through by touching the screens' arrows at the sides. As they ordered up, the pirate knights and officers ordered meals from the carnivore menus. The meals were buffalo steaks, zebra thighs, alien-type sushi, strange big fish, and different meat patties from a cattle or a bison. Tiblo even joined the idea and ordered a zebra thigh. Manda, also joining the menu, ordered one of the giant strange-looking fish. Skinamar and Shana looked on the herbivore menu. There appeared to be meals of leaves, grass, and odd-looking vegetables and fruits. Skinamar ordered the mango-like fruit shown on the menu. Shana ordered a plate of bushel-like grass bathed in a tasteless oil-like substance. Martino and Regulto, as humans, looked on the omnivore menus.

This seems hard to decide, Martino thought. The omnivore menus had random foods to eat such as sandwich foods, vegetarian appetites, and combined foods, usually with grain products such as a crust for pizza or pies.

Martino ordered a burger that contained beef from a buffalo. Regulto ordered a long sub sandwich with shredded steak and lettuce. As soon as all the orders in the restaurant were taken, the screens moved back into their hatches on the ceiling. Suddenly, the door opened. There was Count Joustiáño.

"Greetings!" he said to the freedom fighters with the pirate knights and officers. "Allow me to introduce myself, freedom fighters. You may have gotten my message. My name is pronounced, dehr-maht'so hoos'tee-AHN'yo."

"That's an interesting name," said Skinamar.

"Indeed," said Joustiáño as he continued his story. "My planet of dragons around the Thuban system speaks all kinds of earthly languages: Spanish, French, German, Italian, Dutch, Portuguese, Russian, you name it."

Martino raised his hand from the right side of the table. Joustiáño saw him and said, "Yes."

"You're the dragon that Zinger Warsp told me about," Martino said. "You're the only master who betrayed the lioness, Nala Boomer." Joustiáño was surprised to hear the story.

"Indeed I am," he said. He spread his arms to show pictured holograms that suddenly appeared around the table. There was Nala Boomer as a cub and Joustiáño's relatives.

"Ooh, look!" Skinamar said as he witnessed a picture of Nala Boomer as a cub with her family. He seemed excited about it. "There's Boomer. And she looks cute on all fours, and she has a family, her parents before they died." He looked around the table, climbing out of his chair looking at the pictures of dragons. "Wow, look at all these dragons."

Joustiáño called to Skinamar, "Stupid ape! Get back to your seat!"

"Yes, sir," said Skinamar as he saluted to the count and skimmed back to his chair.

Joustiáño explained his relatives as he showed the pictures, "My father, Rogo, my uncle, Marroncho[1], and my grandfather, Ciango[2]."

1. The double "r" (rr) in the name, Marroncho is Spanish, allowing the reader's tongue to roll his or her "r". Erre=er'r'reh.
2. The "C" at the beginning of the name, Ciango, is an Italian soft "c", which makes the "ch" sound.

Then he flew over to the pictures of Nala Boomer's story.

"You see, freedom fighters," he said. "That lioness was never meant to be any apprentice of mine in the first place. But I had to train her for battle and then leave her prison for her execution."

"So that's why you cheat for a villain," said Martino. Joustiáño chuckled.

Suddenly, a message by the monitor played, "Attention, dinner is served." All of the ordered meals were carried by floating robots. They all knew who ordered each meal as they stood by the right customers. After the robots placed every meal on the table, they left the restaurant.

"Bon appétit," said Joustiáño as he left through a doorway.

A pirate knight was about to dig in his steak. Suddenly, General Fang slammed his fist on the table and shouted, "BOW YOUR HEADS!" The Serpential pirate knights and officers, and even the freedom fighters folded their hands on the table and set their heads over it. General Fang said grace for the food: "Our greatest creator, we thank thee for this great food, for we have starved for it, and we thank our great emperor for his creation and our eternal immortality. We never lose. Amen."

"Amen," said everybody else. They all started eating.

"I've hoped nobody felt anorexic," said Skinamar, eating the fruit he ordered.

"What?!?" said the other freedom fighters.

"Never mind," said Skinamar. They continued eating. The freedom fighters were curious about how strange the food tasted. As they tried it, they ate every bit of it.

After a while, dinner was over. Everybody finished their meal. The freedom fighters were to talk with the officers, Waternoose, and Joustiáño outside the restaurant in the hallway. The conversation began.

"You've impressed me the way you fought our dinosaur guardians," Joustiáño said to Tiblo.

"I am a fierce fighter," said Tiblo.

"So I see," said Joustiáño. "You left your family to die, didn't you?"

"Neither my father nor my brother would ever join you guys," said Tiblo.

"Indeed not," said General Fang.

"And . . . allow us to introduce our bounty hunter," said Joustiáño. Carpoon appeared by the general.

"I'm Carpoon," he said.

"What are you, some parrot-beaked amphibian-looking thing?" asked Tiblo.

"I'm a turtle with no shell," Carpoon said. "I lost my shell when a truck ran over me back on my island. It was just before the emperor had chosen me."

"A turtle with no shell?" said Shana by the others a few feet away.

"I'm frankly a snapping turtle," said Carpoon.

"So I see," said General Fang.

"And what is your purpose exactly," said Admiral MacFnurd.

"My purpose is to find these freedom fighters," said Carpoon, "a tiger, two humans, an orangutan, a kangaroo, and a wolf from another planet."

"So much for our stories in this nightmare," said Tiblo.

"You'll have a piece of us," said Martino to the Serpential officers.

"A deal," said Joustiáño.

"That's enough," said the general. He called the scale troopers who arrived at the talk.

"The tiger is the first for the colosseum," said Joustiáño.

"Take him away!" the general commanded the troopers. And they took Tiblo out of the building to lower ground somewhere away. The general confronted the other freedom fighters.

"Now as for the rest of you, famous freedom fighters," he said, setting his four arms on his sides and opening and closing his hands by tapping each opposite finger with each other. "It was rather nice of you to join us for dinner." His large, stiff tail wiggled. "I hope you don't mind if we show you some of our hospitality."

Floating robots surrounded among the freedom fighters. Electric spires existed on their undersides. They shot their lightning on them and the freedom fighters were suddenly unable to resist. They could no longer move. The electrocution put them to sleep. The officers took the freedom fighters into the dungeon behind them. The freedom fighters remained asleep.

CHAPTER 19

MECHANICAL ESCAPE

Hours passed as the freedom fighters were in dead sleep. Suddenly, Martino was the first to awake by himself.

"Huhhh," he gasped. "We're imprisoned."

Skinamar and Regulto awoke next.

"Marty?" said Skinamar as he opened his eyes. He looked around. "Oh no, we're in a dungeon! And the Serpential officers have vanished."

"Don't panic," said Martino. "We'll have to find a way out."

Manda and Shana were the last two to awake.

"Way out?" asked Shana. "Where are we?"

"We're in prison," said Martino.

"Where is Tiblo when we need him?" asked Manda as she stood up.

"We'll have to find him as soon as we find a way out," said Martino.

Skinamar looked around and found a hatch on the bottom of the wall opposite of the dungeon's gate.

"There's a way out!" he shouted.

"What's going on?" asked Manda.

"We've been asleep since floating robots electrocuted us," Martino explained.

"This is an outrage," said Regulto.

They all went to the hatch. Martino pulled the bricks out and found a hidden tunnel. The freedom fighters crawled inside. First went Martino, then Skinamar, then Manda, then Shana, then finally Regulto.

Meanwhile back in the desert, Zinger and the Invisi-Bot had a feeling that the freedom fighters would not return.

"If my calculations are correct," said the Invisi-Bot, "the freedom fighters will never return if they are already dead."

"They're not dead," said Zinger. "I sense they are imprisoned and soon to be destroyed."

"Oh my," said the Invisi-Bot, "I better contact the federation." He called the Heaven Federation on his wrist communicator. He reported about the freedom fighters about to be executed by the Serpentials. After that, he readied the Great Red Shark and pulled a lever on the dashboard that started its engine. Zinger hovered aboard and the ship started to hover above the ground and then it flew away toward the building, in which the freedom fighters were taken into.

Meanwhile, back in the building, the freedom fighters' way out of prison led to a dark tunnel with red dirt walls framed with steel buttresses.

"It's dark in here," said Regulto.

"Stay with me, everyone," said Martino.

Suddenly, at the end of the tunnel in front of them, there was an entrance of lava-red gases that led to an inside factory. The freedom fighters entered it. The doors opened. Inside were machines melting metal from heated rocks and making parts for droids. Conveyor belts were moving the parts from a tower-like container and sparking machines put them together as bodies. Far below was a storage pit of lava.

"How about that for luck?" said Skinamar. "It's only a factory."

"It might be dangerous to go in," said Manda.

"All we need is to find a way out," said Martino.

Suddenly, a bridge moved forward underneath where the freedom fighters stood. Martino took steps on it all the way toward its end. He looked below it. The highest conveyor belt was nearby.

"It's safe," he said. He jumped on the conveyor below. It led to a nearby metal box. Manda panicked with her paws over her face when Martino jumped on the conveyor.

"I'm next," said Skinamar. He galloped along the bridge and followed Martino's footsteps to the end.

"Be careful, Skinamar," said Manda.

As Skinamar jumped on the conveyor below, Shana went next.

"I gotta try this," she said. She hopped along the bridge afterward. Then Manda went. Regulto stayed behind for a while. Suddenly, Rufus the beast's voice emerged into his mind.

"Forget your fears, Regulto," he said. "Seek the courage to follow your friends." Regulto listened to him and did what he said. He walked along the bridge and then all five freedom fighters were on the top conveyor. Martino witnessed a band of droids coming after the freedom fighters. There were nin-droids, droids that fought like ninjas; jump-droids, droids that could leap into the air to other platforms of a land; cop-droids, droids that flew in the air with helicopter blades; and spee-droids, droids with a wheel-like structure allowing them to run across a terrain, landscape, or floor.

"We've got company," said Martino. The freedom fighters grabbed their weapons out of their packs. They aimed for the approaching swarm of robots. The cop-droids put their tiny foot claws by each other to create an electric zapping beam from back to front. The box at the end of the conveyor was full of scrap metal about to be dumped in a lava pool below. Martino shot one of his disk launchers at a cop-droid. Manda jumped onto a lower conveyor. Skinamar stretched his arms out to grab hanging hooks held on chains from the ceiling. Shana shot one of her boomerang launchers, which launched a boomerang that knocked away several cop-droids. Regulto followed his alter ego's word in seeking courage by jumping to the next conveyors one by one. Martino remained on the end of the top conveyor. Jump-droids leaped into the air toward him and stood on towers at the ends of other conveyors. They aimed around for enemies and launched missiles at their targeted enemies first in the air then toward the conveyor belts by the freedom fighters. Martino leaped to the next conveyor. Manda jumped in a giant metal pot carried by a crane that moved towards the liquid metal dispenser. As Skinamar witnessed it far below him he dropped himself from a chain hook he held on the ceiling. He suddenly inflated himself into a balloon by putting his fingers in his mouth and blowing hard in his own body. He slowly landed on the conveyor by the liquid metal dispenser that poured hot molten metal into the carried pots. The pots were then carried and dumped into a drain and the metal was hardened into new robot parts and particles. Nin-droids emerged amongst Martino. He shot one of them with his disk launchers. Another droid threw its clawed hand like a boomerang that demolished one of Martino's disk launchers. The nin-droids escaped and fled.

"Ow!" Martino said as he got shocked by his destructed launcher. "Great, one of these days," he sighed, "Tiblo's gonna kill me."

And so, Skinamar found a switch on the conveyor by the pouring faucet of metal. He went to it as Manda was being carried towards it. Skinamar quickly activated the switch and turned off the pouring faucet as Manda was carried under it. Suddenly, the whole factory turned off.

Meanwhile, Regulto finally touched solid ground after jumping down from the lowest conveyor. Then so did Shana after she used moves by dodging droids and towers. Martino looked down below and witnessed a pile of black dust far below. He took a breath of air, grabbed his nose by pinching it shut and jumped into the dust from the conveyor he was on as if he were jumping in a swimming pool. Skinamar grabbed a wrench out of his pack and stretched his arm up to the handle of the pot with Manda. He used the wrench to unbolt the handle. The pot fell to solid ground below. Manda trembled out. Skinamar leaped to the ground without breaking any bones. Soon, all of the freedom fighters gathered together. Martino rose out of the pile of dust he jumped in, coughing and wiping the dust off his clothes. He waved his hands around his body to brush the dust off his face and out of his hair.

Suddenly, spee-droids emerged from hatches in the walls. Martino dodged them, avoiding to trip on them. Then so did Manda and Skinamar. Regulto ran by a nearby tunnel that was used as an exit from the factory. Martino threw his damaged disk launcher at the droids that sped in a circle. The electric waves electrocuted the droids until they exploded into smithereens.

"Good riddance," said Shana.

"Good job, Marty," said Skinamar. "That ought to teach 'em."

"Come on," said Martino as he led the others to the tunnel where Regulto stood by.

And so, the freedom fighters walked through the dark tunnel that was thought to lead outside. Suddenly, a net was shot from a gun that grabbed all the freedom fighters and held them inside. It was Carpoon with the net gun. He dialed his wrist communicator to contact the Serpential officers.

"I found the fugitives and I have them captured," he said.

"Excellent work," said General Fang talking to Carpoon's hologram in a communication system column.

"Now, we must crucify them," said Admiral MacFnurd.

"As you wish," said Carpoon. "Carpoon out." He turned off his communicator. He grabbed the giant net with the freedom fighters and through it in a barrow-like loader part of a sleigh wagon. He drove it out of the tunnel with a two-legged beast of two giant horns and numerous eyes (a bug-eyed beast).

CHAPTER 20

THE CRUCIFIXION COLOSSEUM

Just as Carpoon reached the end of the tunnel, he parked the wagon, shouting, "Halt!" to the monster pulling it. He went behind it and grabbed the net with the freedom fighters out of the barrow loader and dragged it out of the tunnel's mouth.

Outside was an ancient colosseum made of dusty red, jagged rock. On the floor ground of light dirt were six crosses made of stone poles. Tiblo was on one of them with his wrists bound at the ends of a metal bar at the top. Carpoon called some pirate knights. He opened the net with the other five freedom fighters. They crawled out of it. Martino looked around, standing up.

"Where are we?" he asked.

"You are about to be crucified," said Carpoon.

"Oh no!" said Skinamar as he lifted himself off the ground. "It's a renewal of Christianity."

"Relax, Skinamar," said Martino. "Tiblo's up there." He pointed to the cross with Tiblo. Up there he was without his pilot's outfit and only in his under trunks with a urinal tube attached to a tank for storing his urine.

Suddenly, pirate knights arrived with crossbars for the freedom fighters. Some of the knights grabbed Martino. They took away his supply pack and took off his pilot's outfit and left his bare skin body almost naked. They only left on his under trunks with urinal tube and tank. They grabbed his hands and set them on the ends of one crossbar. Then they used mechanical wristlocks that could pin a body on the bar. The locks were put around the bar's ends and over Martino's wrists. A sudden untouchable shock pinned the wrists on the bar.

"Ow!" said Martino as he felt the pinning like staples.

Next, the pirate knights grabbed Skinamar, doing the same thing with the other freedom fighters.

"This is sacrilegious," said Skinamar as the pirate knights put his hands to each end of another bar. They put the same kind of wristlocks over Skinamar's wrists.

"DAAAUUUUGGGHHH!" Skinamar screamed as he felt the locks' pinning.

And so, each freedom fighter's clothing was taken off and they were left in their under-worn material. Martino, Skinamar, and Regulto were left in their under trucks with urinal tubes and tanks, as Manda and Shana were left in their plastic breast covert plates and diapers.

And so, the freedom fighters were all pinned on the crossbars, and the pirate knights used pulleys with chains and hooks on the poles to pull each freedom fighter up to the top. And all the freedom fighters were being crucified.

"Where have you been?" Tiblo asked Martino next to him on the crosses.

"We found a way out and tried to escape," said Martino, "but we got caught."

"Now we must relax," said Skinamar.

"I'm not afraid to die," said Manda.

"Well, *I* am," said Regulto.

Meanwhile, the colosseum had an audience of raptors, reptiles, and therapsids that originated from the Death Scale. The announcement balcony was occupied by the Serpential officers along with Darth Waternoose, the twin vulture viceroys, Count Joustiáño, and Carpoon. Emperor Sharp was on a certain mission to a distant planetary system that he barely began. There were four neighboring tunnels in which some pirate knights were building monstrous, robotic, beast-like killing machines for destroying the freedom fighters. As soon as they finished them, Count Joustiáño gave an announcement.

"And now," he began, "since these Heavenly Federal freedom fighters have come this far against us, I give the honor from our emperor since he hired me! I have the honor to use my specialties to back them up!"

"This is going to be a cinch," said the viceroy twin brother Hooker.

"We will win this time," said his brother, Blunt.

"Now!" Joustiáño continued, raising his arms. "Let the crucifixion begin!"

Suddenly, the killing machines were sent out of each tunnel with one. Four of them appeared. One was a brontosaur-like beast with slim, jointed legs and a bird-like head. Another was a prehistoric hoofed mammal (or toxodon)-like machine with curved horns on its cheeks and a large, bulky body. Another was a mechanical mutant rodent with hooked claws, six legs, four eyes, and two rat-like tails. The last one was a snake/dragon worm with two arms with razor-sharp clawed hands. The pirate knights released the killing machines to destroy the crucified freedom fighters. Under the Serpentials' control the machines roamed ahead to the crosses. The hoofed mammal killing machine charged and ran into the cross with Martino. The cross's pole broke and Martino fell on the machine.

"Whoa!" said Blunt in the balcony. "That was nifty."

Martino suddenly, with all his might, broke free from the binders on the cross he was on. The cross slipped down to the dirty ground. Martino drove the hoofed mammal machine to the side tunnel where Carpoon last parked the wagon to get his clothing back. The reptilian worm machine with two arms slithered around the cross with Manda. She broke free from the binders that held her and quickly turned her body around and hung on the cross's bar.

"She can't do that!" complained Hooker.

Suddenly, Martino drove the hoofed mammal machine back, with his pilot's outfit on, into the colosseum. The reptile worm machine coiled its segmented body up the cross with Manda. Manda swished her tail as she tried swinging the rest of her body around the pole. She used her hind limbs to hook together on the other side of the pole. The reptile worm machine suddenly used its razor-sharp claws to cut Manda's back. She shed some blood. Martino used the hoofed mammal machine to roam and ram the reptile worm machine away, knocking it aside from the cross with Manda. Manda dropped herself on the hoofed mammal machine behind Martino. Martino drove the machine to the tunnel he went in so Manda could get her clothing back.

As Tiblo witnessed the new idea with Martino and Manda, he broke his paws free from the binders holding him on the cross. The bird-headed brontosaur machine squawked as it surrounded the crosses. After Tiblo broke free from the cross, he jumped on the bird-headed brontosaur machine, trying to control it. The rodent machine used its hooked claws to grapple around the pole of the cross with Shana. Shana was frightened, she could not break free. Martino and Manda rode the hoofed mammal machine with Manda dressed back in her tunic. As the rodent machine tried to climb up one of the crosses, Martino rode the hoofed mammal machine to run over the rodent machine and break the pole with Shana. Tiblo ran to the tunnel at the side to get his clothes back. Skinamar suddenly got the idea. He slid his hands out of the binders that held him on the cross and dropped down and landed back on the dirty ground. Martino freed Shana from the cross by breaking the binders with his boots. Skinamar skipped and followed Tiblo to the tunnel at the side to get his outfit back, and then so did Shana.

Meanwhile the killing machines started repairing themselves as Martino and Manda rode on the hoofed mammal machine around the colosseum. The last freedom fighter on a cross was Regulto, afraid that he would die without his clothing in the colosseum. He suddenly remembered his alter ego's words and broke free from the binders that held him on that cross. He fell down to the dirty ground and ran to the side tunnel for his outfit.

"Must stay . . . courageous," he said while running.

Meanwhile in the announcement balcony, the Serpentials realized the freedom fighters' intelligence.

"How brave of them to escape crucifixion and get back dressed," said Waternoose.

Blunt flew up and perched on the balcony's fence.

"That's got to be the funniest thing I've ever imagined," he said.

"So, it would seem," said Joustiáño.

"I'm calling the droids," said General Fang behind. He pressed the button on his spiked wristlock to communicate the droid factory and ordered some droids.

As that happened, the freedom fighters were all dressed in their outfits. They fired their weapons at the killing machines. Tiblo flipped around with his twin blasters firing at the rodent and reptile worm machines. As he kept firing, he jumped on the hoofed mammal machine behind Manda as Martino steered and controlled the machine.

On the balcony, Hooker flapped his wings in anger and hovered in the air.

"This is not how it's supposed to be!" he shouted. "Carpoon! Finish them off!"

"Why should I?!" asked Carpoon. "They're just having fun, aren't they?"

"Patience, gentlemen," said Joustiáño, "patience, they will die."

The freedom fighters continued fighting the killing machines. Skinamar used his sunray phaser, whose shots melted down any planetary material, to fry the reptile worm machine until it was destroyed.

"Ha, hah!" Skinamar shouted as he won that part of the battle.

"One machine down," said Joustiáño, "three to go."

General Fang ran to the balcony's fence and spoke in a nearby microphone shouting, "Pirate knights! Attack!"

More hatches suddenly opened on the colosseum's ground circle walls. Serpential pirate knights raged all over the place. Skinamar, Shana, and Regulto fought against them, as Martino, Manda, and Tiblo still rode on the hoofed mammal killing machine and knocked away many pirate knights. The remaining killing machines went wild in a rampage as nobody could control them. The bird-headed brontosaur machine and the rodent machine raged among the pirate knights and half of the freedom fighters.

"I gotta help the others," said Tiblo as he jumped off the hoofed mammal machine.

Suddenly, a swarm of droids emerged from the colosseum's hatches. Cop-droids filled the air, jump-droids leaped everywhere, spee-droids zoomed across the dirty ground, blowing clouds of dirt in their path; and nin-droids provided kung fu among the rampage. A cop-droid hovered toward the hoofed mammal machine and pressed its lower appendages and made an electric beam that made Martino and Manda jump off the machine.

"Ha!" said a nearby bipedal lizard pirate knight. "Those heroes have now lost control." So the hoofed mammal machine roamed free.

Meanwhile, up in the sky flew the Great Red Shark. Zinger and the Invisi-Bot had contacted the Heaven Federation. The federation's pilots arrived over the planet then by the colosseum. General Gando Grizzle appeared behind the balcony's back curtain. He entered where the Serpentials made the announcements.

"Serpentials," he said.

"General Grizzle," said Joustiáño. "What a pleasant surprise."

"You're the one who denied Nala Boomer, aren't you," said the general.

"I am," said Joustiáño as he lifted his helmet and grabbed his light saber racked on his horns. He lit it. "How about a quick duel?"

General Grizzle grabbed his bazooka from a sheath on his backpack. Joustiáño swished his light saber. The general shot a rocket from his bazooka. Joustiáño dodged it by flapping his wings, jumping in midair. Carpoon took out his flamethrower from his supply pack and activated a burst of flame. The general ran from it as it followed him. He leaped over the balcony's fence and fell all the way to the dirty ground below. He then panted in a tiring way.

Tiblo found him while firing his blasters. He ran to the general.

"General Grizzle!" Tiblo called to him. "What are you doing here?"

The general tried lifting himself up.

"I came because of a call from your ship," he said. He finally lifted himself with his bazooka pressed on the ground. "Let's get back to business."

Tiblo went back to fighting the pirate knights, droids, and killing machines. The rodent killing machine was after some of the freedom fighters. Tiblo shot it repeatedly. General Grizzle launched one of his bazooka rockets at that machine. It was blasted into spare parts.

"Two machines down," said Joustiáño, "two to go."

Meanwhile, Heavenly Federal starships arrived in the sky over the colosseum. Soldiers dropped from them on elastic cords. They arrived among the audience and fought with guns around the Serpential beasts and entered the colosseum. Carpoon jumped over the balcony's fence and joined the battle by falling to the colosseum's ground. In the battle, the hoofed mammal machine roamed and rammed at several of its enemies. It almost his Martino and Manda, but they dodged it as it continued running wild.

"I thought that thing was your friend after all," Manda said to Martino.

"No," he said, "I lost control of it."

Pirate knights waved their deadly weapons as the Heavenly Federal soldiers fired their blasters. Carpoon used his bounty scanning visor to use a green pair of lenses and used the targeting reticle to locate the freedom fighters and scan them. Suddenly, the hoofed mammal machine roamed toward Carpoon. He dodged the machine by rolling in a barrel style on the ground. He pulled out his blaster as the machine turned around. It ran back to him and Carpoon shot it repeatedly. The machine slid on the ground and died out.

"Three down, one to go," said Joustiáño.

As Carpoon finished scanning all six of the freedom fighters, he had descriptions made on their pictures. Meanwhile, the last killing machine still active was the bird-headed brontosaur machine. It swung its head by curving its neck among the fighters in the colosseum. Tiblo leaped on its back. The machine turned its head to him. Tiblo shot his blasters at one of its eyes. Just then he dug inside the machine's back by opening a hatch lifting up a metal plate. He plunged his paw inside and disconnected the electric wires. They shocked him for a minute as the bird-headed brontosaur machine turned off and fell apart to the ground. Tiblo leaped free from electrocution.

"Woo!" he said. "Nine lives."

Meanwhile, General Grizzle still fought his way around the colosseum. He knocked away pirate knights and droids, using his bazooka. Suddenly, Count Joustiáño approached the balcony's microphone and shouted "CEASE!" Everybody in the colosseum stopped fighting.

"I have a message to say," said Joustiáño. "General Grizzle!"

General Grizzle turned to Joustiáño above.

"You have fought gallantly," Joustiáño continued, "enough to save your own heroes. You shall win the honor of joining our empire as slaves."

"We will not be slaves under any order of yours," said General Grizzle. "This war is over."

"I'm sorry," said Joustiáño. "But the war has just automatically begun."

The henchmonsters that the freedom fighters fought before came to join the battle.

"Showtime!" they shouted.

There were Lava Lobster, Monstrous Slug, Clown Coach, and others.

"It's clown time!" said Clown Coach.

"Slime time!" said Monstrous Slug, bursting out a train of slime out of his mouth.

"Time for some respect," said Lava Lobster. He used his pincers to plunge into the dirt and created fiery geysers away from him by other fighters. Heavenly Federal soldiers were scared away.

"Argh, ha ha ha ha, Arrrgh!" Lava Lobster laughed.

As the monsters did their duty, General Fang jumped down from the balcony into the colosseum. General Grizzle confronted him as Fang growled.

"Karchong Fang!" General Grizzle shouted. Fang turned to him. Grizzle continued, "My fight was meant to be with Emperor Sharp, not with you!"

"Then your fight IS with me!" Fang shouted. Both of the generals took out their weapons. Grizzle readied his bazooka. Fang had two light sabers and two blasters. He held them in all four hands each. He readied his blasters and lit his sabers, and used them in an "X". He fired his blasters as Grizzle dodged the shots. Fang swished his light sabers. Grizzle fired his bazooka and Fang blocked the rocket with his light sabers. Just then, Fang turned off his weapons and put them back in his belt's sheaths. He ran to the colosseum's wall with the balcony and used his tiny, needle-sharp claws on the tips of his fingers to climb the stone wall back up to the balcony.

As Fang climbed all the way up there, Joustiáño had a bright idea; he wished to run from the freedom fighters, leaving them behind. The Serpentials went below to their ship hangar bay, which was underneath the colosseum.

Just then the freedom fighters escaped through the arch walls of the colosseum's theater. They found the Heaven Federation's space fighting ships. Below the edge was the hangar bay's mouth where the Serpentials got into their ships and zoomed out. Count Joustiáño had a handled, hovering speeder that allowed him to rest on his belly and steer anywhere fast. And so, they all flew out and away.

CHAPTER 21

DESERT CHASE

Just as the Serpentials left the hangar bay, the Great Red Shark was flown in front of the cliff near the freedom fighters. Zinger Warsp showed himself from a window.

"ZINGER!" Martino called out. The door on the ship's side opened. Zinger buzzed out and flew toward the freedom fighters.

"Hello and howdy," he said. "I made a call with our allies to help you break free."

"Thanks," said Martino.

"We must follow the Serpentials," said Manda.

"We'll need carrier transporters," said Zinger.

Carrier shuttles that fly through the sky with passengers came by. Zinger had ordered them. One shuttle hovered toward the cliff and the freedom fighters climbed aboard. The carriers and the Great Red Shark flew off.

"If Joustiáño escapes," said Zinger, "we will lose him before we can get to him."

Tiblo dialed his wrist communicator and contacted the Invisi-Bot.

"Invisi-Bot!" he called as the Invisi-Bot's hologram appeared.

"Yes, Captain," the Invisi-Bot said. So he flew the Great Red Shark to a distant part of the planet. The carriers started to chase the Serpentials.

"We need to find Count Dermazzo Joustiáño," said Tiblo to the pilot of the carrier with the freedom fighters.

"Right away," said the pilot. "I'm on it." He pressed a button on the dashboard that powered up the engines. The carrier went fast.

Meanwhile, the desert was filled with fighting droids and monsters. Machines were powering up and being lifted. Revived prehistoric beasts invaded the territory. The carriers launched missiles at the hovering globe machines that were being carried to the sky. Tiblo called the Invisi-Bot: "We must head for a volcano where I sought Joustiáño will wait for us. Fly over there!"

"Yes, Captain, right away," said the Invisi-Bot. The Great Red Shark was being flown to a distant volcano by speed of the powered engines.

The carriers had wasted many missiles in their path destroying things that tried to attack the ships. They split away. Suddenly, General Fang was sent to find the carrier with the freedom fighters and shoot it down. He maneuvered his globe-headed ship and searched around the Heavenly Federal carriers for the right one. He kept searching.

Meanwhile, the carrier with the freedom fighters zoomed ahead of the desert rampage. They finally reached Joustiáño's path. He sped straight ahead on his belly-resting, handled speeder. His wings were spread out, allowing him to strafe from side to side as he advanced the desert plains and jagged rock walls. Martino went to the front of the carrier by the pilot. The left gunner's pod was next to his position.

"It's Joustiáño!" Martino exclaimed. "Just shoot him, will ya?!"

"We're out of missiles, sir," said the left gunner facing Martino.

"Well keep following him," said Martino, "we'll get to him."

"We're going to need help," said Manda in the back.

"Don't worry," said Tiblo. "We're freedom fighters, we'll face him off when we get there."

Suddenly, General Fang zoomed behind and finally found the right carrier with the freedom fighters.

"Uh oh," said Skinamar as he noticed the ship behind the carrier out the back window. "Bogey on our tail!"

Regulto next to him grabbed a pair of binoculars from his backpack and looked out the window behind him. He zoomed in.

"It's General Karchong Fang!" he said.

"He's gonna kill us!" shouted Skinamar. The general shot his ship's rapid lasers at the tip of the carriers' engine bar.

"We're gonna die!" Skinamar shouted.

Zinger hovered over the passengers.

"Zinger," said Martino. "Where are you going?"

"I'm gonna get help," said Zinger, "the rest of you stay aboard." He flew off the carrier and down to a nearby station with a gunning system.

General Fang continued to fire at the carrier. It rocked side to side and some passengers fell off their seats.

"I'm going to take care of him!" said Skinamar. He jumped out a nearby window and stretched his arms to grab onto General Fang's ship.

"Skinamar!" Martino shouted. He ran to the side and showed his head from a window. He saw Skinamar on top of the ship behind the carrier.

"Don't worry, Marty!" Skinamar called to him. "I'm impervious to violence! WOAH!" The general's ship lowered then hovered. Skinamar shook his head to wake himself up. ". . . and pain!"

The carrier went ahead.

"We might have to stop the ship at one of these moments," said Martino.

"No, Marty," Tiblo snapped at him. "If we stop at one of these points we'll fail our mission." Martino breathed hard as Tiblo continued his message: "We can't let Joustiáño get away, otherwise we'll lose him."

"I know," said Martino. "If I just borrow a bungee cord or something, it'll take just a few seconds or so."

"Marty, we don't have time," said Tiblo. "Skinamar will take care of himself."

"We can't just leave him behind," said Martino. "He's our friend!"

"Listen, Marty!" said Tiblo. "Throwing yourself away from us will get you expelled from the Heavenly Federal Academy. So stay with us. I'm sure he'll come back in a jiffy."

"Alright," said Martino. He breathed more slowly.

Back where Skinamar was on General Fang's ship, he used a tiny piece of broken metal from his backpack to carve the ship's windshield open.

"Elastic demon primate," said the general. "Get off my ship!" He tried shaking his ship by steering it around in a zigzag, diamond, or circle shape.

"WOAH! WO-OHH!" Skinamar shriveled as he tried hard to hold onto the moving ship. As he did, he was somehow launched up as the General moved his ship up sharply. Skinamar's arms stretched as his hands grappled onto the edge by the top of the windshield. He fell back down and broke the glass dropping inside the general's cockpit.

"No chances, evil general!" he said getting up on his feet. "You're going down!"

The general growled he raised his four arms. He slammed one fist on the dashboard.

"You're a joker . . ." he said as Skinamar dodged his fist. ". . . you're a myth!" the general continued talking as he slammed another fist that Skinamar also dodged.

"You're trash!!" the general slammed another fist fast and directly on Skinamar. Suddenly, Skinamar lifted up the fist. He was barely conscious with a black eye and top fur waved up.

"I had said that I was impervious to violence," he said. He stretched his arm and reached for a button and pressed it. It opened the windshield and the general's seat shot up like a rocket into the sky. Skinamar started hopping from ship to ship around the desert's midair. As soon as General Fang reached the sky on his rocketed pilot seat, he jumped down from it and performed a skydiving stunt down to the desert. He landed on a giant globe. He used his tiny claws the stick into the globe's walls and climbed to the top. He took out his blasters and held them in his right arms. He tried aiming for and shooting Skinamar everywhere who leaped from ship to ship below. Skinamar finally went back to the carrier with the freedom fighters.

"I'm back!" he said.

"I was worried about you," said Martino. "But at least you're still in one piece."

"It's true," said Skinamar. "I told you I was impervious to violence."

Meanwhile, General Fang's ship fell to the desert grounds and fell apart in half. Later, Joustiáño had finally stopped at the volcano ahead.

"Stop the carrier!" Tiblo shouted at the pilot. So the pilot carefully landed the carrier on a flat spot. Tiblo had witnessed where Joustiáño had stopped. The freedom fighters walked off the carrier.

Meanwhile, Zinger was at gunnery building and some of the officers were near commanding an attack on the droids and beasts terrorizing across the desert. One of the officers, the commander, a gray canine, showed up by Zinger.

"The desert is clear, Mr. Warsp," he said.

"Well done, Commander," said Zinger. "Bring me a ship."

"Right away," said the commander. He called for a carrier on his wrist communicator. A while later, one arrived and Zinger boarded it by hovering with his wings fluttering.

"I need to find the freedom fighters," he said. The carrier's pilot flew away to where the freedom fighters stopped toward the volcano where Joustiáño had gone to.

CHAPTER 22

MORE HENCHMONSTERS

And so, the freedom fighters scrambled on the desert terrain toward the volcano. Joustiáño hid somewhere inside. Suddenly, a group of newly hired monsters arrived. There were Beard Face, a hairy viper with a horse mane and a human beard; Moosamoosa, a brown-spotted, fierce cow that can spit milk-white acid; Oilteralo, an otter with a flexible body of a black oily substance; and Octavhiss, a snake with eight eyes on tentacles.

Beard Face and Octavhiss alternately struck at the freedom fighters. Tiblo flipped backward. Then he took out his blasters and shot repeatedly. Manda used her instrument, the Silver Harp, to succumb Oilteralo. She took out her zooming arrow crossbow and shot one arrow. Oilteralo quickly ducked under. Moosamoosa spat her acid that dissolved some sand in the ground. Martino shot his disk launcher at that monster. Moosamoosa drooled with her acid on the sand and it dissolved. Oilteralo coiled his body like a snake. Then he uncoiled fast, splattering oil like a sprinkler. Regulto used his cannon-like bazooka and shot a blast that blew the sand in front of the monsters. The sand fell on them. The freedom fighters scattered ahead to the volcano to find Joustiáño.

Minutes passed, they got tired of running across the desert. Tiblo set a paw on a nearby rock at the volcano's foot. The volcano had been extinct, unable to erupt, for many years.

"Joustiáño is hiding somewhere inside this volcano," said Tiblo. He witnessed a cave's entrance up the next level. "We must go in there and find him and confront him."

"Do you think it's safe?" asked Manda.

"Sure it's safe," said Tiblo. "This volcano has been dormant for years. It can't erupt again."

"My thoughts are ahead of you, Tiblo," said Martino.

"Mine, too," said Skinamar.

The freedom fighters climbed up the rock steps to the next level and entered the cave.

CHAPTER 23

JOUSTIÁÑO'S BATTLE

As soon as the freedom fighters entered the volcano, Tiblo led the others through rocky tunnels. As they walked, Tiblo dialed his wrist communicator vocalizing a message: "Mission log, we have come into a volcano in search for Count Dermazzo Joustiáño . . ." The volcano started rumbling and an avalanche of rocks blocked the pathway ahead. ". . . uh, negative, we have a several roadblocks. Tigro out." Tiblo turned off his communicator.

"I've got a stupid feeling that we won't get out of here for a while," said Skinamar. The freedom fighters stopped at a junction between a slope uphill and another one downhill.

"Now which way do we go?" asked Martino.

Tiblo looked around and tried guessing where Joustiáño must have flown.

"This way," he said pointing at the slope. And so, the freedom fighters started climbing up the rocky slope.

"This seems quite difficult up there," said Manda.

"Urgh!" Shana stressed as she climbed and followed the others. "What makes you so sure about this, Captain?"

"I'm a tiger," said Tiblo, "I'm always sure."

Suddenly, a rumble happened, causing the volcano to quake.

"The volcano's unstable!" Tiblo shouted. "Everyone hold on!"

"Th-this is-ss b-bad!" Skinamar said as he shook, holding onto the slope.

"We must hold still or we're done for," said Martino.

"My tail is thumping," said Shana as her tail tapped the slope.

"Hey, wait!" Manda called out. "It's not the volcano." She witnessed a shadow moving by the cave exit nearby the trail. "It's a ship moving on it!" She was right. A large ship moved on the side of the volcano. It landed on a platform above the cave's mouth. It was Carpoon's ship. He climbed out of it and entered the cave nearby. Back inside the cavern, Tiblo confronted a wall.

"No time to lose," he said. He reached in his backpack and grabbed a rope, long enough to hold more than one individual. Tiblo tied it to one of his booted paws. "Grab an end, somebody."

Martino grabbed a segment, then Shana, then Manda. Tiblo pierced his claws into the rock wall and started climbing.

"Eh, Captain," said Skinamar, "why don't we have me stretch my arms up there?"

"We'll be expecting that later," said Tiblo as he continued climbing. Martino, Manda, and Shana held on tightly to the rope. Tiblo carried all three of them up the wall with all his brute strength.

Meanwhile, Zinger had a carrier ship approach the volcano. The Great Red Shark was landed on the other side.

"Thanks for the ride," said Zinger to the pilot, "I'll take it from here." He fluttered his wings and flew toward the volcano in search for the freedom fighters.

And so, back inside the volcano, Tiblo made it all the way up to the top of the wall. He untied the rope around his boot and pulled Martino, Shana, and Manda up the wall. Martino got up first. He continued to help pull up the females of the crew.

"My paws aren't strong enough," said Shana. She was about to slip down the rope. She grabbed it between her jaws. Manda was brought up next.

"We need to help Shana get up," she said.

"Help keep pulling," said Tiblo and Martino simultaneously. Manda helped pull the rope until they finally got Shana up to the ledge. Shana put herself on the floor behind the ledge feeling exhausted.

"Thanks for the help," she said to the others.

The remaining two freedom fighters below were Skinamar and Regulto.

"I got a wonderful idea," Skinamar said. He had Regulto grab one of his hands. Skinamar stretched his arm up to a stalactite far above. All of sudden, he and Regulto zoomed up to the stalactite. Skinamar's face was pressed hard against it. He and Regulto dropped down from it and rejoined the others.

"It was a fast ride with him up here," said Regulto.

"Thank you," said Skinamar, brushing his arm fur.

"Come on," said Martino.

"This way," said Tiblo. The freedom fighters followed Tiblo into the next cavern. They went through a large cave mouth. There were ponds of lava on the left from the entrance. Suddenly, a hanging object fell from the ceiling and folded its wings hovering in the air. It was Count Joustiáño.

"You freedom fighters have come to the right place to challenge me," he said. He lifted his helmet and grabbed his light saber from being racked on his horns. He lit it was a bar of red light. Tiblo went first and took out his blasters. He fired repeatedly as Joustiáño waved his light saber side to side fending off the blaster shots. One blaster shot was bounced back at Tiblo it hit him at his shoulder. He bled. He backed up against a wall. Martino was next.

"Ah!" said Joustiáño. "A few humans working for the Heaven Federation, eh?"

"Well, I am a slow learner," said Martino as he took out his remaining disk launcher. "I heard that you betrayed Nala Boomer."

"That was because I had to quit having her and join evil because of my traits of a dragon slash reptile," Joustiáño said.

"Then you're under the Serpent's Ghost," said Martino. Joustiáño swished his light saber. Martino shot his disk launcher.

"Marty!" Tiblo interrupted. As Martino turned to him, Tiblo tossed one of his blasters to him and Martino caught it. He used both the disk launcher and the blaster to face Joustiáño in battle. Skinamar suddenly decided to sneak past the fight and stretched his arms up to the cavern's ceiling and grabbed a stalactite. He swung from stalactite to stalactite.

Back in battle, Joustiáño raised his light saber about to perform a counterattack. Martino snuck under him while Joustiáño was in midair. Martino cut his leg with a sharp part of his disk launcher.

"Ah!" Joustiáño shouted a bit. Then he laughed. The wound on his leg shed an oily substance instead of blood. "As a Serpential I have a circulatory system of oil. Besides, I have no true blood to shed." The wound was repaired with tiny robots building a metal scab.

"Well, only we, freedom fighters, do," said Martino. He fled the fight and joined Tiblo whose shoulder needed to heal on the rock. Manda went next to fight Joustiáño.

"I show off nobility, Count," she said. "My father had shown me when I was a whelp."

"So I see," said Joustiáño.

Manda grabbed out her crossbow with zooming arrows. She launched one and Joustiáño dodged it. He flapped his wings and swished his light saber. Manda defended herself with her crossbow. Joustiáño chopped it in half with his light saber. Manda put her front paws together to perform a prayer. Joustiáño sliced off her paws. Manda opened herself from the prayer of failure.

"Victory is mine, freedom fighters," said Joustiáño as he pointed his light saber at Manda. He turned it off. He walked to Manda's back. "I can steal any courage or nobility from you, Miss Monka." He bopped the butt of his light saber on her head. Manda fell to the floor. Suddenly, Skinamar activated his klaxon that made ape sounds. Joustiáño was distracted. Shana took a boomerang from her pack and threw it by Joustiáño. Joustiáño blew fire from his mouth. Regulto joined Martino and Tiblo resting on the rock nearby.

Just then, Zinger flew by the cavern following the freedom fighters' footsteps. He entered the cavern and confronted Joustiáño as he confronted Zinger.

"Ha ha!" Joustiáño made a laugh. "Zinger Warsp, my insect friend. It's been years since we first met."

"It's also been years since you abandoned your apprentice, Nala Boomer," said Zinger. He used the tips of his jointed legs to form a force shield that can be used as a remote-controlled flying disk. He tossed it and it zoomed like a Frisbee. Joustiáño swished his light saber at it. Sparks were made when the saber touched it. The disk flew back to Zinger.

"I hear you've become powerful as I imagine in my small brain," he said.

"I have become more powerful than any freedom fighter," said Joustiáño. He expelled lines of lightning from his claws. "—even you."

As Zinger caught the lightning with his jointed legs, he absorbed it within his body. He shot the lightning through his stinger back toward Joustiáño. Joustiáño dodged it. He and Zinger continued fighting. This went on and on with Joustiáño's light saber and Zinger's flying disk. The freedom fighters watched the battle. Zinger and Joustiáño were both dodgy to each attack. The next time, Joustiáño clanged his light saber on Zinger's disk, Zinger made a block of defense.

"What great strength that you've provided," he said.

"This is where we draw," said Joustiáño. He and Zinger backed away from each other. Joustiáño turned off his light saber. Zinger widened his jointed legs and the flying disk vanished.

"Catch me if you can!" Joustiáño called to the freedom fighters. He started flying through a tunnel behind him next to a fall of pouring magma. The freedom fighters started to follow the path next to him. Zinger used his legs' power to form a lava proof footboard that Tiblo jumped on.

"The rest of you head through the tunnels to the exit!" he commanded the other freedom fighters. "I'll take care of Joustiáño right here!" He took out his blasters; one of them was given back to him by Martino. Tiblo aimed his blasters at Joustiáño.

"Bon voyage!" Joustiáño said, turning himself face-to-face to Tiblo. Tiblo fired his blasters repeatedly. Joustiáño kept himself in the air over the running lava. Tiblo kept balance on the board as it was washed along the way. The other freedom fighters followed the side tunnels, running the whole path in zigzags and curves.

"This can't be good enough," said Martino as he panted running through the tunnels with the others.

"We'll have to keep moving," said Manda as tears came to her eyes as the running went on. Zinger followed the crew behind.

A while passed; the tunnel exits were reached. The freedom fighters in the left tunnel ended up in a tunnel that allowed them to fall through until suddenly, they fell in water after a long fall. They found a secret passage under the water's surface on a lower wall. They went back up to the surface. Meanwhile, Tiblo reached another exit with a lava fall as Joustiáño flew away by Carpoon's ship. Tiblo sky dove toward the river below that was ahead of the cooled lava falling in water. Back in the cave, the rest of the crew made a deal.

"Alright," said Martino. "We're going to swim through that tunnel below. Everybody take a big breath to hold."

"I don't think I can swim," said Shana.

"It's easy, sort of," said Skinamar. "All you do is, when you're underwater, to stroke your front limbs and kick with your back limbs."

"I don't have my front paws to do this," said Manda.

"Just follow my lead," said Martino. He inhaled a large amount of oxygen from the air. Then the rest of the crew did it. They all dove underwater, following Martino down to the way out. Zinger flew down the tunnel following them down to the water. He formed an air shield around himself. He sank into the water and down to the tunnel as the freedom fighters found their way out. Zinger flowed through the tunnel and found the freedom fighters at the exit. Tiblo was just ahead. The others swam up to him.

"Did you get him yet?" Martino asked about Joustiáño.

"No," said Tiblo. "He escaped."

Suddenly, way up in the sky above, Joustiáño pulled out a flare of yellow fluid from his belt. It was mustard gas.

"Hasta la vista, freedom fighters," he said. He lit the fuse on fire with his fiery blow. He dropped it far below to the ground on a shore next to the river where the freedom fighters gathered. Zinger flew ahead to find the Great Red Shark. The flare reached the ground.

"What is that?" Martino asked as he noticed it. The flare shed the gas evaporating out of it.

"That's mustard gas," said Tiblo, "we can't inhale it." The flare exploded.

"Swim away!" Tiblo commanded the others. Everybody swam down the river as soon as the mustard gas spread. The freedom fighters later ended up in a stream that washed them all the way to a lake at the end. On the other side was the Great Red Shark. The freedom fighters swam toward it. Zinger was waiting for them as he hovered in the air with his wings fluttering. The crew climbed out of the lake and walked to the ship. The ship's conveyor reached the ground from the entrance. The Invisi-Bot walked on it downward, happy to see the crew.

"Your ship awaits, Captain Tigro," he said.

"Leave it all to me," said Tiblo. "I'm taking it from here."

"It's right where you want it, Tiblo," said Zinger as he followed the freedom fighters on board.

As soon as everyone climbed aboard, the door closed and the conveyor slid itself up in its slot. Tiblo flew the ship way from the planet.

"Zinger," said Skinamar, "you were awesome when you shot that lightning out of your stinger."

"Yes, indeed," said Zinger. "Years ago I had my poison gland removed and I collected powers to overcome dangerous tasks with my mental magic. I even use it to make tools and weapons."

"Wow," said Martino. "You must have been on a lot of adventures, especially the ones you told me about, Zinger."

"I need handicaps to replace my paws," said Manda. "Joustiáño sliced them off."

"Don't worry, we'll get to that idea," said Tiblo. He flew the ship out of Geodou's atmosphere along with other surrounding ships to reunite with the Heaven Federation.

CHAPTER 24

THE AFTERMATH REPORT

Meanwhile, Carpoon flew his ship away as Joustiáño rode on it. They headed for Serpentopolis as the Death Scale was nearly completely together. It needed its southwestern section. Carpoon and Joustiáño rode into the south building's hangar. They met with Emperor Sharp, back from his mission for a while, and Darth Waternoose. Carpoon and Joustiáño climbed out of the ship they were in.

"How was everything?" asked Emperor Sharp.

"The freedom fighters shall admit defeat," said Joustiáño.

Carpoon got a scan of the freedom fighters on a chart. He showed it to the emperor. Tiblo's face had a subtitle saying "The Leader". Martino's subtitle said "The Curious One". Skinamar's subtitle said "The Crazy One". Manda's subtitle said "The Shy One". Shana's subtitle said "The Smart One". And Regulto's subtitle said "The Coward".

"My bounty hunt is a success, your majesty," said Carpoon.

"Excellent work, Carpoon," said the emperor.

Suddenly, flashes of screen spark appeared nearby. It was General Fang with some pirate knights. They had a Heavenly Federal male canine pilot, tied in plastic cords and gagged.

"Your majesty," said General Fang to the emperor. "We found the traitor."

The emperor turned to the general as one of the pirate knights threw the pilot forward. The general untied the gag from his mouth.

"Emperor Hieronymus Sharp," the pilot started talking.

"Your name," said the emperor.

"Diggs," said the pilot. "Morris Diggs."

"What was your purpose of your federation?" the emperor asked.

"I tell the history about human children stories that were written from Earth to all my partners."

"So I see." The emperor contacted the scale troopers on his wrist communicator. "Troops, we have an enemy in the south hangar. Arrest this pilot."

"Right away," said one of the troopers. He turned off the communication and the emperor's hologram vanished. The scale troopers walked to the south building's hangar. And so, back there came the new ideas and plans for destruction.

"I suppose the biosphere will need more power," said Darth Waternoose to the emperor.

"As soon as it is complete," said the emperor, "we'll be ready to crush our enemy." He walked to a shuttle nearby with a group of guards in red silk robes. "Now," said the emperor, "I must return to my mission."

"Good luck, your highness," said Joustiáño.

The emperor climbed aboard the shuttle he rode on. The guards followed him. The scale troopers arrived to take Morris Diggs to the detention level. The shuttle with the emperor started to take off. The engines burned and the shuttle flew away. It left the Death Scale's atmosphere. It was destined to a distant world.

CHAPTER 25

MANDA'S HOSPITALITY

For Manda's missing paws, Tiblo flew the Great Red Shark to the Heaven Federation's hospital ship. He called for some doctors and told them what happened with his wolf maiden. And so, the freedom fighters were led to a room on level 3 by a tall robot on wheels. They had Manda lie on a bed. Her arms were set on the blanket by the side edges.

"Just relax, Manda," said Zinger hovering over her. "Hold on to your patience."

"I am patient," said Manda.

The robot turned to the others and said, "Her bionic paws will take 3 to 4 hours to complete." It moved ahead to a room where handicaps were made. Professor Fester Whiskey was there making the new paws, burning metal and drilling sparks in certain sections. Suddenly, Jer the tapir arrived.

"Captain Tigro," he said. "Good to see you again."

"Hey, Jer," said Tiblo.

"Trouble with one of your scouts?" asked Jer.

"Yeah," said Tiblo. "Manda has lost her front paws, so she'll need handicaps." He decided to stand next to Manda to watch over her. Suddenly, memories came to his mind from when he trained Manda and Shana when they were very young. There were challenges of combat and flying.

Meanwhile, moments passed, the handicaps were halfway done. Some of the freedom fighters sat with Jer. Manda fell asleep on the hospital bed. She began to dream something. The dream had a monster fighting against her while she had her handicapped paws. She used a laser-powered cutlass to slice the monster's jointed legs. The monster opened its jaws with sharp, jagged teeth and made a loud scream. Suddenly, Manda jumped up from her sleep and gasped deeply. Skinamar jumped and went toward Manda.

"Don't worry," he said. "Calm down, I know CPR."

"She doesn't need CPR," said Tiblo. "She has a hard time relaxing it seems."

Meanwhile, Artidector appeared by a window.

"Freedom fighters," he said, "failure happens to everyone, especially those whom I had worked with before. When I was a mortal, I helped all sorts of heroes around Earth to achieve their destinies. But as a god, I helped Nala Boomer reach the boughs of the Death Scale. I had Joustiáño take care of her for me. I thought he would be a good master for Boomer, but I was wrong. After all, Joustiáño is a villain. He always worked for the Sharp Empire."

"Oh," said Martino. "I had no wonder about that. He is just a dragon."

"Hey!" Skinamar shouted. "I figured it out. That foreign name, 'Dermazzo Joustiáño', must be equivalent to someone named, Dermott Joustyear, because there are Spanish words like 'justa' meaning 'joust' and 'año' meaning 'year'."

"Very clever!" said Jer. "I figured that from studying foreign languages of Earth on the Internet."

"Smart brains you have," said Shana. "Just like me."

"Another clue," said Tiblo. "Joustiáño said he had no true blood to shed. He is a Serpential because of the circulation of oil. But we have true blood. As heroes, our blood becomes a true responsibility to every heaven."

Jer got up from sitting on a plastic bench and giggled. "That's an interesting story, Captain," he said.

"He's right, you know," said Zinger, sticking on a pole connecting the floor and ceiling.

A moment later, the handicaps were complete. Professor Whiskey gave them to the tall robot on wheels. The robot moved to the freedom fighters with a tray that had the handicaps.

"Handicaps for Miss Monka's paws are complete," said the robot.

"Oh, good," said Tiblo. The robot turned to Manda. It grabbed her arms.

"Right arm," said the robot, letting go. Manda lifted her right arm and the robot started to attack the right bionic paw on the tip. The bionic paws were silvery, shiny handicaps with flat digit front sides. The saddle joints had sliding sticks holding up the digits from slots.

"Left arm," said the robot. Manda reached her left arm and the robot connected the left bionic paw on the end.

"You are complete," the robot said.

"Thank you," said Manda. She got up from the bed and rejoined the freedom fighters. "I also need a new weapon. Joustiáño destroyed my crossbow."

"We'll worry about that later," said Tiblo. All the freedom fighters looked at the stars outside the window. Suddenly, the Invisi-Bot came by.

"Oh, heavens!" he murmured. "I seem to be low on oil as I found you all." He saw the freedom fighters staring out the window into space. "I see Manda Monka put back together again."

"Yes indeed," said Manda. "Look at these bionic paws." She showed the Invisi-Bot her handicaps as she was able to control them by moving the digits.

"At least we're back together as an upright team," said Martino.

"I'll give you some oil, Vizzy," said Skinamar. He scampered to the couch and the Invisi-Bot followed him to a distant room. The rest of the freedom fighters stayed to watch the stars.

THE END

WITH TRUE BLOOD COMES TRUE RESPONSIBILITY

As Tiblo said about Joustiáño being a Serpential, having no blood is having no faith of heroism. Any animal with real blood has a right to obey the reality of courage. Any creature with an oil system shall not use blood but use a pump inside it rather than a heart.

Other info:

"Eye to Eye" from Disney's *A Goofy Movie* found in Chapter 1